Iceberg Tips

Soheil Nashtahosseini

A Novel

Copyright © 2021 Soheil Nashtahosseini All rights reserved

The characters and events portrayed in this book are fictitious. Any similarity to real persons, living or dead, is coincidental and not intended by the author.

No part of this book may be reproduced, or stored in a retrieval system, or transmitted in any form or by any means, electronic, mechanical, photocopying, recording, or otherwise, without express written permission of the publisher.

ISBN: 9798530305771

Imprint: Independently Published

Cover design by: Soheil Nashtahosseini

Dedication

To my wonderful and caring parents, my lovely sister and brother-in-law, my sweet nephew, my dear relatives, and my amazing friends for their kind presents, and special thanks to my longtime dearest friend and editor. I also want to thank anyone who directly or indirectly, even without knowing, helped me throughout my life.

Table of Contents

Chapter 1 .... *1*

Chapter 2 .... *19*

Chapter 3 .... *30*

Chapter 4 .... *40*

Chapter 5 .... *52*

Chapter 6 .... *60*

Chapter 7 .... *72*

Chapter 8 .... *81*

Chapter 9 .... *95*

Chapter 10 .... *102*

Chapter 11 .... *113*

Chapter 12 .... *122*

Chapter 13 .... *132*

Chapter 14 .... *143*

Chapter 1

An old gardener was working on the balcony of the Grinsteins. Dr. Richard Grinstein was an obstetrician, and his wife, Dr. Sara Grinstein, was a Transplant Surgeon. They lived in a luxurious house. The old gardener had a large pair of hedge trimmers in his hand to trim the boxwoods, and he bent his head to check, like a hairdresser, that the branches were cut in the exact same size. Inside the house and in the reception area, overlooking the balcony, Richard and his wife were having a party with their close friends. They were a couple, around forty to forty-five years old, very fashionable and wealthy. They were also well-known doctors in their field. Among their friends present at the party were Dr. Randall Hershberger, an anesthesiologist, and his wife Johnna, a housewife. They looked like a happy couple. The third couple at the party was Damen Hague, a famous and reputable Attorney, and his wife, Dane, a schoolteacher. Rumor had it that Damen also worked with a gang of professional criminals and assisted them in legal matters. His wife, Dane, was suspended for a short time. According to her, it was for mistreating a student. But she tried to make no one, but Damen know it. Richard always told his wife, Sara, "It is a great advantage that as physicians, we have a good lawyer for a friend to help us with legal matters because you never know which of your patients is also a mental patient and complains about you for the service they received!" Little did Richard know that Sara and Damen had a secret affair for a long time!

The last person to attend the party was Lieutenant Deputy Chief of Police Jonathan Hodge, who was usually very quiet and listened carefully to what others had to say, sometimes uttering a few words to ignite a conversation. Jonathan was single and had recently divorced his second wife. Damen, Richard, Randall, and Jonathan were close friends since college. They used to live in the same house. While on the balcony, the older man could hear the sound of talking and laughter. But he was just busy doing his job until Damen, as usual, joked with him to entertain the crowd. Mr. Ghiaccio was a man of many talents. Damen was, in fact, a clown and always liked to make his friends laugh at the expense of others. But Mr. Ghiaccio was a 60-year-old man with an elegant appearance.

Damen said jokingly, "Hey old man, have you ever cut someone's hair with those hedge trimmers?!"

Richard added, "Oh, that is scary!" Then he jokingly turned his eyes to Damen and laughed.

"I bet he can cut his child's hair with the same hedge trimmer he is using to cut these boxwoods neatly!" Said Damen, "They are trimmed so neatly!"

"It was an embarrassing joke!" Johnna said defensively and seriously, "Never joke about someone's child!"

"Ask him to cut your hair down there, with the hedge trimmers! Maybe I saw something there! You know what I mean!" said Dane, sarcastically.

Damen and Sara glanced at each other and smiled mischievously. And although Damen felt embarrassed, he acted as if what Dane said didn't matter, "Yep, okay!" said Damen. To change the tone, Randall said,

"Oh, why did you make the conversation so dangerous and scary?!"

Ghiaccio turned to them and, in a wise but charming tone, replied,

"What you said is not scary. Do you want me to tell you a horrifying story that won't let you even close your eyes at night to sleep?! My story is probably the scariest story you have ever heard because it is a true story! It's not like the Ghostbusters and the Cottage of Horror. I assume everyone has seen those movies. Some people may have laughed to themselves at the naivety of those scared of watching them. They are right. Because those movies are based on completely fictional stories. But my story ..." Ghiaccio took a deep breath and said with great sadness, "Unfortunately, it is completely true!"

Damen felt that it was turning into a serious affair, so he said, "Who is this guy?" Sara gazed at her husband as he examined the situation. Johnna jumped up and clasped her hands very innocently, and said, "Yeah, storytime!" Richard turned to Ghiaccio seriously and assessed the situation, then said,

"It's only been a couple of months that you've worked for me. We just hired you, and we do not even know you well!" He emphasized the word 'just.' Then, he paused for a moment and said surprisingly,

"You have only come here a few times, as far as I know, to take care of our trees and garden. That's all. Besides, you did not even get permission from us to enter our friendly gathering. If you are going to work for me, you have to keep the boundaries and know your place!"

"But you talked to me and started the conversation, and it was rude to ignore you and your guests. I wanted to entertain you with an interesting story. But you are right. I'm going back to work," said Ghiaccio respectfully.

He then went back to the balcony where he was working. He continued to trim the boxwood with his large scissors. Richard thought to himself,

"I taught the new gardener a lesson and successfully controlled the situation!" He returned to his friends and continued talking to them.

"I bet his story is as boring as he is!" Damen told the crowd with a burst of proud laughter.

"But I wanted to hear his story!" said Johnna.

Randall, who had a very controlling personality, angrily looked at his wife to silence her. Johnna was fully controlled by Randall and looked down and stayed quiet. It was clear that she was both upset and not having much fun in the gathering.

"I don't have a problem on my part," Richard told the crowd, unhappy with the unpleasant friction that had formed between them. He continued, "My only problem with him was that he came to talk to us without permission! If the group agrees, we can tell him to come in and tells his story and entertain us!"

"It's great!" said Randall in a playful tone, "Let's have a game and bet on it! After he finishes his story, we can decide if it was boring! But before that, we have to vote. I bet $400 that his story is interesting and true!" Randall secretly wanted to please

3

Johnna after he made her upset. He looked at her when he finished his sentence.

"Let's double it!" said Richard, proudly.

"I bet one grand that he is going to be boring, and I know it! And you know I am always right!" said Damen.

Richard looked at everyone and asked, "One grand, does everyone agree?"

They looked at each other and said, "Yeah, sure!"

Johnna jumped up again and shook her hands childishly and said, "Yeah, storytime!"

Richard got up and picked up a notepad and a pen from inside a small table next to the room. He wrote everyone's names on it, and in front of his name, he wrote 'not boring.' He then handed the notepad to Randall to write his bet and give it to the next person down the line. Only Damen wrote boring. If he lost, he would have to give a thousand dollars to each present in the room. Of course, this amount did not bother him, and even for others, that amount was like a change in their pockets. But betting was their habit of making everything they did together more interesting and adding some Spice to their activities! Richard looked at his friends, got up and walked over to Ghiaccio, and said,

"Hey, I wanted to apologize to you for treating you a little badly! I did not mean to insult you. We want you to come in and tell us your story. Of course, that is if you still want to! No pressure!"

Ghiaccio looked at him and hesitated, and said, "Okay, why not!" He dropped his tools and went into the hall with Richard. There, Richard turned and sat down in his chair.

"Hey everyone, my name is Ghiaccio," said Ghiaccio, "Nice to meet you all! Good! The story I want to tell you has nothing to do with fairy tales or haunted house adventures. There is no room for superstition! Of course, you have to listen to it till the end so that you can put the puzzle pieces together. In fact, this story is a fully documented and real story that happened in January 2010 on the Italian island of Sicily. I am about to tell you about events that have a different type of thrill to them, and there is no understandable explanation for them!"

Everyone moved in their chairs to make themselves comfortable, and it was clear that everyone was intrigued. Ghiaccio continued,

"Of course, I will tell you the location of the place and the name of the neighbors of the house where these events took place so that if you have any doubts about the truth in what I say, you can go to that house and inquire from those neighbors, who are aware of the story to some extent."

It was clear from the audience's raised eyebrows that they were even more surprised! Damen, who voted against the story, leaned forward a little in his chair and looked around in disbelief! Ghiaccio continued,

"To ease your curiosity, let me just say that none of you are as pessimistic and skeptical as I am! When I first heard about this, I mocked the speaker and assumed that I heard fantasies about some imaginary people! However, evidence and clues about the accuracy of these rumors gradually emerged from every corner and changed my mind! Eventually, my acquaintance with the adventures that took place in the house at No. 17 on La Punta dell'Iceberg turned my life upside down. When I heard this house's story, I did not believe it and thought that everything had emanated from my friend's dreams and that he just wanted to scare me! But from the moment I went to my friend's house and saw the trees in the yard from the window, I became fascinated and realized there was something unusual about this story. It was so bizarre that it could not have been the work of someone's imagination! I was told that the first person who told the story was a friend of the house owner. It is said that after the incidents in that house, she went crazy and was hospitalized in a mental hospital for some time. That's how I got involved in this story to some extent. Because I had a newspaper reporter ID card, I contacted the local police department and asked about the house's homicides."

"Are you a journalist?!" asked Johnna, in surprise.

"Yes, retired, I have been in different parts of the world for years. And this story is about the time that I was working in Italy," Responded Ghiaccio.

"So why are you a gardener now?" asked Dane, "A journalist at your age shouldn't need to work."

"Everyone needs a job. I have always wanted to be a gardener during my retirement. This way, I only deal with plants and trim diseased plants and remove the dried ones from the ground. I had only one son, who died four years ago, and two years later, my wife died because of grieving over my son's untimely death. I could not stand being alone, so I entertained myself with gardening." Said Ghiaccio. Everyone looked at him and said, "We are sorry for the loss of your family!"

Ghiaccio said nothing and was silent for a moment. Then, Sara said in an insensitive tone,

"Tell us the rest of the story!"

"Where did I stop?" asked Ghiaccio.

"Because you had a press card, you went to the police station," Johnna said with her usual kindness.

"Oh, yes. They gave me as much information as they could. And that was almost the equivalent of nothing!" said Ghiaccio.

"What did the police say?" asked Jonathan.

"They denied the murder and said that the only report they had was one case of insanity and six cases of disappearance. I did not get any useful information from the place of work of the only survivor of that event. Everyone said that she was a rational and intelligent person before that incident. They never saw any sign of madness in her. I was stonewalled, so I decided to find the survivor, and after a lot of inquiries, I found her. She lost her faculties and was hospitalized," Ghiaccio replied.

"Too bad, she must have been so traumatized," said Johnna.

Randall gently put his hand on his wife's leg and said, "These are temporary states. These things happen after painful events. It can happen to anyone!"

Ghiaccio said, "I'm sure she was a powerful woman, but she could not find her strength at the time. However, I often traveled a long way from my house to that psychiatric hospital to interview this person and gradually gain her trust and convince her to tell me her story. When she did, I was sure she was just delusional! It was obvious to me that the story could not have happened the way she described it. However, apart from the story, she talked with great insistence and shunned people in the story. She said that she lost her trust in humanity. After that, she no longer showed any signs of insanity. I recorded her words on tape and then stopped going to the hospital. I was so confused and was just frustrated with the story. Then, I received an unexpected gift! For some unknown reasons, the only survivor of that house sent me a thick notebook of her notes through a hospital staff. Apparently, I was able to gain her trust during my interviews. The obsessively written booklet contained details of the survivor's conversations with other family members and friends. Many people went missing in that house, Dr. Umanita's house, and accurate data about all those who spent that mysterious night there was in that booklet. Even the exact mood and conversations of the people involved in the story were described in that booklet in great detail. Although everything seemed unreasonable, I did not give up! I interviewed Dr. Umanita and all the neighbors in that alley separately. Among these neighbors was an older man. Apparently, the only survivor of Dr. Umanita's house knocked on his door and was in such bad condition that the older man had to let her in, and he took care of her for a while. During this time, she explained the whole story to him. After hearing the details, the older man was horrified for some time to the point that he would get afraid if someone approached him.

The older man said it was as if a force was compelling her to speak about the horrible events of that night. He remembered the story exactly. The older man's words helped me understand what happened in that house more accurately, especially since the only survivor of the story had forgotten an important part of the story due to trauma or was just not willing to talk to me about it.

After talking to the older man and looking back at that notebook, I had a clear and vivid picture of what happened in that house.

It was so weird that I could not believe it, yet I was fascinated by it, and it occupied my mind! I was willing to do anything to find out the truth! That's why once in the middle of the night, I stealthily jumped over the wall and into the yard of house number 17, but to be honest, I did not dare to enter the building. I just looked inside the house through the big door. It was not a matter of being afraid of the house occupants because the owners have either disappeared or been traumatized by mysterious events. The house had long been empty.

However, a terrifying feeling was transmitted to me from the building. Of course, I have to say that I spent many nights on the front lines during the war. Even once, a detachment of enemy forces passed me from a very short distance, but even then, I wasn't afraid as much as I was when I entered the yard of house number 17 that night! It's been about eleven years since then, but every time I think of that night, a cold sweat goes down my spine!

Three years later, I learned that one of the government agencies purchased Dr. Umanita's mysterious house and decided to renovate it as an office building. After that cold January night, no one remembered or didn't want to remember that this was the house in which six people disappeared! Dr. Umanita's attorney also died sometime in those three years. Apparently, Dr. Umanita's will said that if he died and his heirs did not accept the terms of his will, the house was to go to the University of Catania. But the will was lost, and apparently, no one claimed possession of the house. I quickly found the agency in charge and spoke to someone to find out if this was true. The agency's public relations officer confirmed that such a house had just been purchased. The objects inside were to be auctioned off, and the house was to be rebuilt. When I heard this rumor was true, I was petrified! With great difficulty, I found the head of that agency. I made an appointment with him, with a slight misuse of the press ID card, under the pretext of conducting an interview on a subject related to him! When I met him, I asked about the house. As I thought, he knew nothing about the disappearance of Dr. Umanita's heirs. But apparently, he had heard few rumors. He said that the neighbors were superstitious for thinking the house had guardian spirits that prevented thieves from entering. He said that the department's inspector, who went there to visit the place, confirmed that nothing was stolen from inside the big house of Dr. Umanita during the seven years that it was abandoned.

There were valuables in the house, and if a thief were to enter, he would definitely steal many things. The head of the agency did not believe the rumors, though. But he had no explanation as to why the inspector resigned after going to that house and never set foot in that house again. Having entered the courtyard of that house once before, I knew that the case of the guardian spirits and things like that was nothing more than a myth. During the past seven years, and the years before that, many thieves had entered that house, and the same calamity that happened to the six heirs happened to them too: they all disappeared! I cautiously told him the whole story I heard about that house and warned him of the dangers of entering that house. I explained to him what might happen if he took the old, hand-made wooden chairs out of the house, which I was told look like electric execution chairs, and asked him to either leave the house alone or destroy those chairs. There was a great danger lurking there for a very long time, and if it were released, there would be a great catastrophe. The head of the agency listened to me patiently. Still, it was clear from his facial expressions that he did not take the warning seriously.

I know this story is hard to believe. But if you have any doubts about its accuracy, refer to the evidence that I will present to you. Dr. Umanita's house is located on La Punta dell'Iceberg, although I do not recommend entering the large courtyard. Carina Umanita is still in the hospital and will answer your questions if you insist a little. I am well aware of this narrative's unusualness, and I have no explanation for what happened in that house. I do not think this story has anything to do with ghosts or demons. Because the only unusual elements that exist are those dark and inlaid wooden chairs, and they should never be taken out of that house. When I think about those chairs being sold to ordinary people who are unaware of everything and the power the chairs will find in the cities after being dispersed, the hair on my neck stands up! If the chairs come out of that basement, a big catastrophe will happen.

The story began when Dr. Umanita, the eldest of the Umanita family, died. The deceased was one of those healthy older men who lived to be eighty years old. Neighbors said he walked the steep streets around his house every morning until the last days of his life. He died suddenly of a stroke. Everyone said he was wealthy. But when he died, it turned out that he just had a house in the whole wide world. Of course, that one house was considered a great wealth in those days. Dr. Umanita inherited this house from his ancestors. It was a huge house, with a magnificent four-story facade built in the style of the old Italian lords' mansions. The building was designed by the famous nineteenth-century architect Nascita. It is even mentioned in history books that Dr. Umanita's grandfather was a friend of the architect.

The house was located in the middle of a few gardens and groves in the heart of one of Sicily's old streets. Two doors opened onto this courtyard. One of them led to a river by a winding path. Some said that the only survivor of these sinister events threw her relatives' bodies into the river and vanished them, and that is why the bodies of these people were never found. There was another way to enter the house. This entrance was the one that was usually used, and it was at the end of La punta dell'iceberg. At the end of this narrow, tree-lined alley was a large door, with Dr. Umanita's courtyard in front of it, making the alley an impassable deadlock. There were only two other houses in that alley, both of which were as large as Dr. Umanita's house and had large courtyards, but neither was as large as the doctor's house. The house's exterior was made of white stones, and the passage of time had a great impact on the stones' color.

Nevertheless, the house's large windows with wooden coverings and the tall pillars still retained their old glory, indicating that long ago, this house was a majestic palace. The yard was full of dense trees because after Dr. Umanita's gardener's sudden death, the yard was left alone, and it gradually became like a dense forest. In front of the main house and at the foot of the wide white stairs that led to the entrance, a large stone statue was placed that depicted a warrior riding a horse. There was also a large pool in which all kinds of fish swam in the past.

But after Dr. Umanita's death, the water had dried up, and only a few large skeletons of fish remained at the bottom of the pool. Dr. Umanita was isolated in the last years of his life. Before that, he gladly accepted invitations from universities and intellectual circles. From time to time, he met his old students too. But after his first stroke, the right corner of his mouth was paralyzed, and he lost interest in going out and stayed home most of the time. He no longer had the patience to discuss old or new topics with the students. He went to class once and then officially resigned from teaching. He said that the youth of this period and time were different and cursed the inventor of video and the computer games, which in his opinion, made people idiots fascinated by the screen. The pension he received from the university was so small compared to his wealth that he did not even need to leave home to cash his check. Dr. Umanita was an organized and detailed-oriented individual. Until the last day of his life, he followed calculated and accurate plans. He was known for his discipline and accuracy: The grocery seller knew when the doctor would call every other day to put in his order; His publishers knew that his books and articles would arrive on the exact agreed date, And the neighbors knew the exact time he would leave his house every morning to go for walking and to exercise. Everyone admired this aspect of his personality. Also, Dr. Umanita was known to be a kind person. It would not even cross anyone's wildest dreams that he had such a terrible curse hidden at home.

Perhaps, it was because of his discipline that he could think everything through and escape the curse! His lawyer said the doctor was aware of his impending death. Because two days before this last stroke, he called the lawyer and reminded him of a few details about his heirs. Dr. Umanita never got married. It was said that when he was very young, he fell in love with a girl and got engaged to her. But that girl died in an unknown accident, which I have some ideas about. After that, the Doctor lived alone for the rest of his life and never got married.

He also did not have a child of his own to inherit his wealth. All his heirs were the children and grandchildren of distant relatives. Although Dr. Umanita never saw many of them, he compiled a detailed list of their names and addresses and given it to his lawyer, who had to inform them as soon as the doctor died. And that's exactly what his conscientious lawyer did. One morning, the local baker, who served hot bread to the doctor every morning, came across the half-opened courtyard door. At first, he thought the doctor left the house for his usual walk and forgot to close the door behind him. But when he cautiously walked in, he saw the doctor sitting at the stone warrior statue's foot as if looking at the pool. The baker went forward and saw that the doctor was dead. It was as if he felt pain in his chest while walking in the morning and left the door open so that help could appear soon if something happened. Then, he went to the pool and died while casting his last glance at the reflection of the morning sun on the water.

That same evening, the lawyer called the phone numbers on the list and gathered all the heirs in his office on Giustizia Street. Those who gathered that day in the lawyer's office had only one thing in common, and that was the fact that they all had the same last name, Umanita. A number of those who were related to the family on their mother's side also retained the surname for unknown reasons. The day when everyone gathered together was cloudy and humid noon in late December. It was raining heavily, and it was difficult to get to the law firm, which was located in a remote area. However, everyone was there on time. When the last person arrived and was guided by the secretary to the luxurious conference room, he found himself in the company of people that had nothing in common with one another. A few minutes later, the lawyer arrived too and looked at the audience through his thick glasses. Then, he moved his glasses forward on his nose and took a closer look at the list. A professional smile appeared on his wrinkled face, and he said,

"Greetings to the esteemed members of the Umanita family! Fortunately, all the friends who were supposed to be present at today's meeting are here. As you know, I am the lawyer and an old friend of the late Dr. Umanita. As I explained to you over the phone, your names are mentioned as his heir, and it is my duty to arrange for his property to be transferred to you." There was a commotion around the table.

"Excuse me, of course, but I did not know at all until yesterday that I was related to Dr. Umanita!" said a tall, young man, who seemed to be an athlete and was sitting at the far end of the room, "How did he leave me an inheritance? Are you sure you did not make a mistake?"

The lawyer glanced at his list and said with a reassuring smile, "I'm absolutely sure! You are Mr. Renzo Umanita, and your name is mentioned as the heir in the will. I think many of the friends sitting around the table here have never seen Dr. Umanita, and I think at least half of this group members were not even aware of their kinship to him! However, this does not change anything. The deceased carefully identified his heirs' names and addresses, and I act according to his wishes."

"Well, could you tell us exactly what the deceased's will says?" said an elegant young lady with a turquoise necklace protruding from her neckline.

"Of course!" said the lawyer, "But before that, let everyone introduce themselves so that the audience can get to know each other. I think this is necessary because Dr. Umanita addressed this group as a whole. There is a division of property that you have to do together."

Everyone looked confused. It turned out that most of them knew each other as little as they knew Dr. Umanita! Finally, the silence was broken by a man clearing his throat. He was a young man with long hair on his pink shirt and a pair of sunglasses on his head. The young man said,

"Well, if we are going to introduce ourselves, let's start then! Even though I have never seen Dr. Umanita, I have a deep respect for him, and I am not upset to be his heir! Let's get to the bottom of this soon; I have to be somewhere in an hour!"

The lawyer turned to him with a smile and said, "Well, why don't you start?"

"I am Karmelo Umanita," said the young man, as if he was waiting for the offer! "As you said on the phone, I am his cousin's son. I never knew Dr. Umanita. I am a medical student at the University of Catania."

The one sitting next to him was the elegant girl, who wore a necklace of large stones. When it was her turn, she arranged her hair with a movement of her hand. By doing so, she showed the wide bracelet she was wearing, which was decorated with turquoise stones. She said in a beautiful and attractive voice,

"I am Emma Umanita. I study fine arts, specifically painting. My grandmother told me that she had a brother, but I never saw him."

The next person was a middle-aged, short, and overweight man with short grayish hair and a long beard covering his face. He wore photochromic glasses with dark plastic handles and a white shirt soaked in sweat under his armpits. When it was his turn, he said in a loud and pounding voice,

"I am Ercole Umanita. My aunt was the doctor's brother-in-law's sister. I work for law enforcement. Unlike the other brothers and sisters in this group, I had a close relationship with the late doctor and met him frequently. I loved him dearly!"

13

Next, someone sitting by the window in the corner of the table spoke. He was a young man and wore fashionable clothes with good taste and had a notebook open in front of him. From time to time, he wrote things down. He wore gold round glasses and had a short and neatly trimmed beard.

"I am Gino Umanita," he said in a firm tone, "I am a medical student, and I knew the late doctor through other relatives."

Next to him sat the same young athletic man. He had his hands crossed on his chest, and his arms' large and tangled muscles became more visible. He had distinguished cheekbones. His long hair was tied behind his head, and he was wearing a tight blue T-shirt. His voice was deep and resonant, and when he began to speak, everyone turned to him. He seemed to be waiting for Gino Umanita to finish to follow his words. He started with a bit of embarrassment,

"Renzo Umanita. Honestly, I do not know how I'm related to the deceased. The relationship you mentioned over the phone was so complicated that I can't remember! I am a freelancer."

"The doctor's aunt was related to your grandfather," said the lawyer.

The last person, sitting on the other side of the table, in front of Karmelo and near the lawyer, was a young and lively girl who stared straight at the audience with her big, beautiful eyes! You could sense that she was a challenger! She introduced herself with complete confidence,

"I am Amelia Umanita. I'm a medical student. My mother's aunt was related to the doctor, but I never saw him myself."

Next to her was a beautiful and nice woman with innocent eyes. She hesitated for a moment and said,

"my name is Carina Umanita. I never met Dr. Umanita, but I heard from my grandparents that he was a very nice man with a lot of accomplishments."

After that, the lawyer began to speak again, "Well, now it is time for me to inform you of the contents of Dr. Umanita's will. According to the document that he entrusted to me, all seven people sitting around this table enjoy the deceased's property equally. What is left of him is an old house in the Avidita area, with a base of twenty thousand square feet!"

A loud voice arose, "Wow, how many square feet did you say?!" It was Amelia! Everyone looked at her, and she said with embarrassment, "I mean, did you read the number correctly?! Ah, twenty thousand square feet of infrastructure is a bit unusual!"

"No, I said the number correctly. He has a house with a base of twenty thousand square feet, which has four floors on the ground and at least two basements," said the lawyer politely.

Renzo moved in his chair. As the lawyer looked at him, Renzo asked, "What do you mean at least two basements? Isn't it clear how many basements there are under that house?"

"To tell you the truth, I never went to the basement of that house," said the lawyer, "The deceased was very strict about not letting anyone into the basement. He said that even gardeners and servants never went to the basement. That is why no one knows exactly how many floors were built under that house. He wrote at least two floors in his will."

There was silence. It was as if everyone was thinking about a thousand-yard house with several basements that extended to an unknown depth! Finally, Amelia won everyone over by saying,

"Please continue!"

The lawyer continued, "Yes, I was saying that this house also has a yard that covers eighty acres and, in the north, extends to the mountains, with a high stone wall, precisely, four yards high. That's all the inheritance—a house with a yard around it and all the property and furniture in that house. These will be passed on to you seven people with a few conditions."

Amelia shouted again, "What conditions? There is no need for conditions!"

"Anyone that wishes so can sell their share and do whatever they want with the money!" said Gino, sarcastically.

15

The lawyer looked at him sharply and said, "In fact, this is one of the conditions of the deceased. Dr. Umanita set four conditions that must be met when the heirs seize his property. Two of these conditions apply to me, and I will guarantee them through legal documents. The other two are up to you, and morally speaking, you should respect them."

"Now, what are these conditions?" asked Renzo.

The lawyer continued, "The first condition is that the house should never be destroyed, and the yard should remain intact. Trees can be pruned, and yards can be manipulated and planted. Still, no part of it should be destroyed, no tree should ever be cut down, and no part of it should be destroyed for construction."

Complaints erupted around the table. Karmelo said,

"We are surprised! Why does it matter to someone dead what we want to do with our share? Does a wise person leave the land of this size unused? This is a gold mine! we can build a magnificent building in that beautiful land!"

The lawyer ignored the commotion and continued, "Real estate documents will be transferred to you only after you sign a legal document that contains your written commitment to keep the property intact. As soon as a tree in the yard is cut down or a part of the Doctor's house is destroyed, the property will be legally taken out of your possession and dedicated to the University of Catania."

Karmelo, who did not seem to understand correctly, asked, "How can it be?"

Amelia also said angrily, "Wow! What non-sense!"

"I hope I have made the first condition of the deceased clear. The house and the yard should remain intact, and the only renovation of the building and planting new trees and plants in the yard is allowed," Responded the lawyer.

"Well, these are not too bad. What are the other conditions?" asked Gino.

"This is not too bad?! What is not too bad?! What good are a few acres of expensive land if it is not sold?!" said Karmelo.

"The guy owed us nothing! Yet, he left us his property! We have to thank him for making us his heirs! Beggars can't be choosers!" said Carina calmly.

The lawyer took advantage of a moment of silence that followed and said, "Well, the second condition is that the movable property is divided into seven equal parts under the observation of all seven of you."

"Excuse me, what does that mean?" asked Emma.

"It means that your group will own the furniture and property in the house of the deceased in the first stage. And then, you negotiate among yourselves and conclude the division of this property between all of you fairly," responded the lawyer, "Provided that the property that everyone receives will be of equal value, and everyone will be involved in the negotiation process, everything will be done fairly. The first complaint from anyone causes the house to be taken out of the possession of all members of this group."

"What is this condition?! What will happen?" said Emma.

"The deceased wanted to make sure that none of us cheated on the others. Suppose all the negotiations about property division are discussed in front of everyone. In that case, we have no choice but to give everyone an equal share. The possibility of secretly fouling others and double-crossing them will be reduced," said Renzo.

The lawyer smiled gratefully and said, "Thank you for your honesty! I think that is why the deceased made this condition."

"Well, it seems we have to accept these conditions. I do not think they are too bad! But you said that two other conditions apply to us?" asked Emma.

"Yes, as soon as you sign the documents that I will give you and promise to meet the first two conditions, the property will be transferred to your group. Each of you gets a seventh of the value of the yard and land, and you can take possession of the house to arrange the division of property inside the house. You have to meet the other two conditions too, but there is no monitoring of your behavior about those." Replied The lawyer.

17

"Well, what are those two conditions?" asked Karmelo.

The lawyer cleared his throat and said, "The first condition is to block the entrance door to the basement of the house with bricks and cement, and then never let anyone enter the basement. This should be done at the time of your entry into that house. This means that you should not enter the basement, and none of the basement things should be moved. Everything is to remain the way it is left in the basements!"

"Oh God looks like this guy was crazy! Why shouldn't we take out the property in the basement and divide it up?" complained Ercole.

The lawyer said that the deceased did not explain why he made those conditions mandatory.

"The next condition is even stranger!" said the lawyer. Everyone's attention was drawn to him at those words.

"The deceased stated, with great intensity, that there is a set of antique and engraved wooden armchairs in the basement, and no one should ever sit in any of them!" said the lawyer.

"No one sitting in the armchairs?! Why?!" asked Gino with a glare.

"I do not know," said the lawyer, "In fact, this is the strongest testament I have ever encountered during my forty-eight years as a lawyer. But I know Dr. Umanita was so smart and discreet that I am convinced that he had good reasons for this condition. I will now distribute seven copies of the prepared document to you to sign and commit to the first two conditions. Please sign them to arrange a property transfer. The other two conditions are up to you!"

Chapter 2

It took about two weeks to complete the paperwork to transfer ownership of house No. 17 on La Punta dell'iceberg. On the evening of Friday, December 6, 2005, after the administrative work was completed and the certificate of ownership of the house was issued to those seven people, the members of the Umanita family were scheduled to go to Dr. Umanita's house for the first time to discuss the distribution of furniture in the house. It was from there that the relationship between them slowly became more intimate. Since they were all either Mr. Umanita or Ms. Umanita, they decided to call each other by their first names. The members of the group reacted very differently to the last two conditions and their plans for their inherited wealth. Amelia wanted to know the amount of her wealth as soon as possible. She was thinking about selling her share and use the money as capital for a luxurious life. She longed to travel around the world and preferred to venture out with some of this windfall wealth.

Karmelo was also in favor of determining everyone's share of the inheritance and selling them. However, he had no clear plan for the money he was about to receive. He cared so little about the furniture's value that he told the others to go to the doctor's house themselves and just leave a seventh of the furniture for him. Like everyone else, he thought the doctor's furniture was a collection of old, depreciated objects. He did not want to argue with others about such trivial things. Others had the same idea about the furniture in that house. Still, they feared that the absence of one of them on the day of the property division would violate their pledge and that they would lose the ownership of the entire property to the University of Catania because of a dispute over furniture!

For this reason, Ercole and Emma went to Karmelo that evening and took him out for dinner. After a nice meal, they convinced him to go to Thursday's meeting for property division. Ercole and Emma were acting in unison. Emma was completely obedient to Ercole, and everything he said was like Revelations issued by God! Others were less secretive about their decisions.

Amelia found the house pleasant and liked to stay at home and hold her energy therapy and psychic coffee reading sessions under the courtyard's old trees. That's what she did as a hobby! Renzo wanted to rent out his share of the house to his friends for a small price and live with them there. Karmelo was stubbornly silent about his plans. Gino wanted to sell some of his shares and publish the books he had written. Thus, on a fuggy and cold Friday in mid-January, the seven passed one by one through the large courtyard gate of Dr. Umanita's house and joined at the house's main entrance.

It took some time for the seven Umanita family members to find and turn on the yard lights. In the meantime, four of the seven new homeowners passed through the large old trees in the yard that were terrifying at night and got to the building. The last people to walk this path in the dark were Renzo and Emma, who came together. Like the rest of the heirs, they had a key to the house. After entering the yard, they almost ran to the house. Their path was not too dark, as the moon was full and illuminated the courtyard's white trees and cobblestones. But the same pale light made the shadows lurking in the corners of the courtyard's mysterious space look scary. What was on Renzo" nerve was Emma that kept repeating in a monotonous voice that the house was cursed and haunted and that she had just seen something like this in a horror movie!

However, when they saw the dim light next to the front door, they breathed a sigh of relief and calmed down. They were on the threshold of wide white stairs leading to the front door. Others managed to find the electrical switches, and suddenly the courtyard lights came on. The lights were all around the building. The courtyard's depths, which was still dark, looked even scarier in the dim light of these scattered lights. Finally, at ten o'clock at night, all seven heirs gathered at the house of the deceased Umanita. The last person to get there was Gino because he had spent part of his time strolling in the semi-dark courtyard. When he passed the white stairs that looked like a dream under the moon's dim light and opened the house's front door, he was greeted by the welcoming voice of the others. With a bright and playful look, Amelia greeted him.

"Well, my distant relative has arrived! Welcome to the family party!"

Gino was a little taken aback by the warmth! Amelia took off her coat, and her long, wine-colored hair shined on a plain white T-shirt. This Amelia bore little resemblance to the serious, moody girl he saw two weeks ago! Amelia stepped forward and led him to the main hall, where the others sat together. Gino greeted everyone and said,

"Well, looks like you've made yourself home already!"

Jokingly, Renzo touched him in the shoulder with a firm fist as he shook his hand and said while pointing to the furniture, "Seems like they are more expensive than we thought!"

Gino looked at the walls of the hall, on which large and expensive paintings were hung. They had expensive, heavy gold frames. In the middle of the hall was a heavy, inlaid wooden table, and around it was large chairs on which the group was seated. Ercole was standing in a corner away from the others, looking at the crystal objects in the wide display case. Gino looked closely at the texture of the large rug under their feet and said,

"Yes, the furniture must be expensive! This rug alone is of great value!"

Amelia jumped with passion, "Let's all go and see the rest of the rooms! I want to go through this house and look at everything!"

So, all seven of them toured the house. Everyone went to the fourth floor, the highest part of the building, and decided to start their walk through the house and go downstairs. It was as if everyone refused to approach the basement, which they were barred from entering. As Renzo said, the property in that house looked like a small treasure. There were exquisite objects in all the house's countless rooms, objects that resembled a museum's belongings! As if Dr. Umanita's house was a palace that contained the whole history of humankind in it! The heirs first talked and laughed and were happy to own such items! But the more they explored, the less they talked and laughed.

It was as if the value and variety of what they saw weighed on them, and they could not believe that all these things were inherited to them. The plan of the house was so complicated. Room after room was connected to each other, and there were rooms in each hallway connected to other secret rooms. It was so complicated that they thought they would get lost in this maze and soon stopped looking for all the rooms. They decided to go in one direction, so they only entered rooms located in the

21

hallway they were walking through. The house was so large that they seldom passed a room twice. The rooms were all full of different things. They passed a room that was apparently Dr. Umanita's office. It was only then that they realized that this anonymous relative of theirs was a great artist!

The walls were covered with colorful and brilliant paintings. A semi-finished painting on a canvas stood by the window. Emma eagerly looked at the paintings and announced that Dr. Umanita was one of the greatest painters of all times! There was an ebony table on a corner with a complete set of calligraphy supplies. Large paper tubes full of beautiful calligraphy were scattered around the table. But that was not all of it! The more they went through the house, the more they realized Dr. Umanita's wide range of talents! There were shelves full of books in all the rooms, and glass frames could be seen in the corners with beautiful and exquisite objects behind them. They saw a collection of colorful crystal stones, a complete collection of small stone sculptures, and a spectacular collection of old rifles.

There were many stone statues in the corners of the rooms, carved in ancient and mythical figures. Since they were all made of the same dark stone, it could be guessed that a special masonry made them by order of Dr. Umanita. The house consisted of countless rooms connected by winding corridors. The rooms were arranged in all conceivable ways! There was a room in the center of each floor that was perfectly round and had a huge wooden table in the middle. There were glass showcases on the first floor around these rooms with exquisite objects on the shelves. The fourth floor was full of books. It was one of the largest private libraries Gino had ever visited. Renzo and Gino eagerly stopped there, rummaging through rare, old books that were handwritten and piled up on the library's dusty shelves. However, Karmelo and Ercole exploring the second floor, found the central room filled with expensive ornaments and statues. First, everyone thought that the most valuable thing in that hall was the huge engraved copper trays hanging on the wall. Until Karmelo realized that the other gold and silver objects were not plated and were made entirely of gold and silver, this discovery thrilled everyone, as the value of the items in that hall alone was beyond their imagination! Finally, after hours of wandering around the house, everyone gathered on the first floor. That is the place where they first gathered together.

Everyone was tired of exploring the house, and they were sure that there were still rooms they have not looked at. The first-floor lounge seemed empty after visiting the upstairs rooms. Allocating a hall empty of exquisite objects seemed unusual for the house. Everyone sat in that room for an hour and talked excitedly about what they had seen. It was almost dawn, and many were tired and half-asleep when, for the first time, a dangerous offer was made! Gino was the one who wickedly came up with the idea and said,

"Let's go and see the basement, too!"

"What is the use of seeing items that we are not going to take out? It's also in violation of the contract," said Renzo.

"Well, yes, but there's no reason not to ignore it! The will stipulates that we should not take anything out of it and block the basement entrance. Still, Dr. Umanita did not say not to walk around and look at the furniture there!" replied Emma.

"He wrote not to go to the basement, but I have no problem with it unless that lawyer understands we did!" said Renzo, jokingly.

"Now, who wants to let him know?!" said Amelia in a seductive tone, "We are all in the same boat. If someone makes a hole in it, we will all go down; we will all lose this house with everything in it!"

"I think the fact that Dr. Umanita made it a condition to block the basement's entrance shows that he hid something expensive there, and he does not want us to find it!" said Ercole.

"What do you think can be more expensive than gold and silver?" said Renzo, sarcastically, "I'm sure you will not find anything of particular value there."

"But it is certain that we are not going to block the entrance without looking inside. I am not willing to do that!" said Amelia.

"I will not go downstairs with you all because we a made promise not to, and I do not want to be a traitor!" Carina said firmly.

"What a non-sense! he is dead. He won't know it. It means it never happened!" said Amelia mockingly.

23

"Sure, he is dead, but we are alive! I won't come with you. I will wait up here for your return," said Carina.

"We promised to cover the basement entrance without going in," said Renzo, who was tired of walking and was lying in a chair.

"Well, yes, our intention is not to break our promise," said Karmelo, "We just want to take a look at what we are giving up!"

"I don't think there's anything wrong with just looking!" said Gino, "Especially since we know there are at least two basements, I would like to know how many floors are really under this house."

Karmelo happily rubbed his hands together and said, "Okay, so let's go see these mysterious basements! I know the way. As we walked down the first floor, I found a large wooden door with a narrow staircase behind it that went down. I think it's there!" With that, everyone got up and followed Karmelo.

Renzo insisted on being left there to take a nap. Still, the enthusiasm of others prevented him from staying behind. He said he should go to the restroom before seeing the basement. After he returned, his eyes were sparkling, and he longed to see the basement too. They all passed through a long, curved corridor and reached a heavy wooden door with large Greek mythological figures and scenes engraved on it. Gino whispered and said,

"Wow, what a beautiful door! This is a treasure in itself! When we are blocking the doorway, we can take the door out of its frame and sell it!"

Renzo rolled his eyes at him and walked down the stairs. Renzo had already climbed the narrow, damp basement stairs. The staircase that led to the basement was completely different from the stairs that connected the house's upper floors. These stairs were at an angle to each other and twisted around an axis, just like a church bell tower's step. Unlike the rest of the house, this hallway was simple and unpretentious, with light blue walls. The smell of dampness wafted from the end of the hallway, and it was clear that the lower parts of the basement were not properly ventilated. The hallway led to a network of large, spacious rooms that seemed to be based on similar designs to the upper floors. All the rooms were full of different items. Household furniture, such as tables and chairs, some of which were worn out and old, boxes full of books covered with spider webs that no one had touched for years, and boxes full of different objects. The basement ceiling was slightly above the ground level. The pale yard light that filled the courtyard fell through a narrow window. This dim light was enough to see some of the surroundings, so no one bothered to look for the light switch. It looked like a group of pirates had hidden legendary treasures there, and then a severe storm swept through the underground rooms and dislocated everything! The basement was full of the most unexpected things everywhere.

Renzo put his hand into a large box next to a wall near a large bronze lampshade, and, to his surprise, he pulled out four or five colorful dolls. On the other side of the room, Karmelo saw a large, complicated tape recorder and sound mixer. He said,

"Oh well, looks like our deceased relative loved to have fun!"

While looking at the objects in the basement, everyone kept moving forward. Eventually, they passed a big door that led to a huge room. It was the counterpart of the large, central rooms on the upper floors and was full of strange objects arranged in it. In the middle of the room, among various dust-covered objects, were the infamous wooden chairs. Ercole looked in amazement at a dried deer head attached to a beautiful wooden plate hanging on the wall. Emma happily moved a large number of paintings that had been piled up, side by side in a corner, dusting them off before looking at each one. Amelia was thrilled to find a large box filled with pink crystal dishes.

Meanwhile, the first person to notice the chairs was Renzo. He stood in front of them in the same tired state and said loudly, "Look at these! They are here!" The others looked at him. They seemed to have forgotten all about the last paragraphs of the will where it talked about the chairs! Karmelo, across the room, holding a large samurai sword, asked,

"What is there?"

"The same wooden chairs that Dr. Umanita said we should not sit on!" said Renzo.

25

Suddenly, everyone remembered the will! Amelia went to Renzo and looked at the chairs with a curious look. Then she said,

"It is strange that they are a standard set of chairs. Why shouldn't we sit on them?"

"Maybe their wood or frame has a problem, and it might break and tear our pants," said Amelia.

"No," said Renzo, "These are not very normal! You see, there is an inch of dust on all the furniture in this room, except for these chairs, there is no trace of dust on them. Do you see? It's as if someone just wiped them with a damp cloth!"

"That's no reason not to sit on them!" said Emma, "Maybe they look clean because of their dark color. They seem to be made of high-quality wood."

Then she bent down and put her hand on the handle of one of the chairs. But she immediately withdrew her hand and said,

"Wow, it's a bit hot! It is as if a heater is lit inside it!"

Gino joined them, "I want to know why we should not sit on these! These seem very comfortable!" said Gino.

Karmelo laughed from across the room and said, "Hey guys, look what I found!"

Then he showed everyone a brilliant collection of precious jewels that was put in a delicate box. Then, seeing that everyone's attention was drawn back to the chairs, he said,

"My dears, leave the chairs!"

"I'm telling you," said Amelia, confidently, "This was an illusion created by the brain of a superstitious old man!"

"No, that would be the case if these were some common objects that superstitious ideas are usually based on," said Ercole, looking at the chairs with some fear, "But these are not the things that people are usually superstitions about."

Renzo agreed with him for the first time since they entered the house, "Yes, they look quite modern. They look more like electric execution chairs!"

"Right? Do you see? They even have the logo of the chair manufacturer on them. It must be made in Germany because German letters are written on them," said Gino.

"Do you think they're German?" asked Ercole.

Renzo, who was able to find a large number of different swords and daggers in a corner, said, "Guys, let go of those chairs! The deceased said, do not sit on them! Then, we do not sit on them! Let's look at the rest of the cool stuff here! I cannot let go of this collection of old daggers!"

But Amelia seemed more interested in discussing the chairs and said in her usual rude tone, "Let one of us sit on a chair to see what happens! If something goes wrong, the others will not sit on them! I volunteer myself!"

"No, we promised not to sit on the chairs," said Emma, "There must be a danger, so we should not sit on them. More importantly, if one day it becomes clear that we broke our promise, this house may go to the university. Then, we will lose the inheritance!"

"Nothing like that will ever happen!" said Amelia, "Have you forgotten? The lawyer said that when the ownership documents were transferred to us, no one cared about us unless we violated the first two clauses of the contract. He said many times that whether or not to fulfill the last promises is up to us and are just moral obligations."

"True, but that's not the reason. What if we sit on the chairs and something bad happens to us?" asked Gino.

"You mean you really don't want to know why the deceased said we should not sit on these chairs?!" replied Amelia.

"I do want to know!" said Gino, "But I'm thinking about how to do it without putting ourselves in danger. All we have to do is to use an ax and break one of them to see what's inside. Maybe when the woods come off, we see that there is something hidden inside them!"

27

"No, it's a pity to destroy one! These chairs are worth a lot! How can you destroy this beautiful wood with an ax?" said Emma.

"Why not? It's not like we're going to sit on them later!" said Gino.

"Maybe we do to sit down!" said Amelia, under her breath.

"These chairs are German. Maybe they were torture or execution chairs!" said Gino, "The date on them is close to World War II!"

"Maybe that's why he didn't want us to look at them so that this secret would be kept hidden forever!" exclaimed Amelia.

Karmelo approached them from across the room. The sound of his footsteps in the dusty, semi-dark basement was so frightening that everyone was silent for a moment. Karmelo, who seemed to be frightened by the echo of his footsteps among the old furniture of the room, joined the crowd standing in front of the chairs and said,

"Look, I think we need to clear our minds about some things! Do you understand what I mean?"

"No, what do you mean?" asked Ercole.

"Take a look at all these things down here!" said Karmelo, "I mean, do you really want to block the door of the basement and bury all these valuables in the basement?! How can you?!"

Amelia looked with regret at the inlaid wooden frames, and the large collection of painted canvases stacked in a corner and said,

"Honestly, no, I do not like that!"

Renzo shouted from the other side of the room, "I don't like it either!"

"I have an idea," said Ercole, with a sly smile, "We can get all this furniture out of here and then safely block the entrance! This way, we carry out the deceased's will too!"

Emma said, "But it was in the will that we should not take anything out of here."

"Madam, the deceased was definitely mad that he wanted us to do something like that!" said Ercole, "There is no reason for us to do whatever he said! He wanted us to block the door. Well, we will do that. There is no reason to listen to his orders about leaving all these expensive things. right?!" Ercole looked at the others to gain their approval, then continued, "It's a shame to leave all of this here and get the door blocked!"

"If I'm not mistaken," said Emma, "the doctor's intention was not to take these chairs out of here. Well, we can leave the chairs alone and take the rest of the things. What do you think?"

Renzo said in a loud voice, "I agree. Isn't it a pity to leave everything here?!"

"I agree," said Ercole.

Karmelo looked at the chairs with admiration and said, "I'm thinking, why leave the chairs here and go? Well, if no one wants to sit down, I'll take them! I do not mind sitting on these!"

"Well, I want them too! If you want to sit on them, call me, I want to see what happens!" said Amelia.

Renzo coughed and said, "Wait, wait, either we all sit on them, or no one will touch them! Doing otherwise means on the first day, you want to do something that divides us! Either we all break our promise, or no one acts against the will!"

"We now own this house and everything in it, and we can decide on our inheritance. Isn't it true?!" exclaimed Ercole.

"We have not seen all of this basement yet," said Gino, "As the lawyer said, there is at least one more floor below us. Let's continue our tour and then take the opportunity to decide on this. Do you agree?" Everyone agreed.

Chapter 3

They scattered around the basement again and began to mingle around. All the rooms were covered with old and dusty furniture. The sun was now completely up in the sky. The light coming in through the half-window near the ceiling shined through the walls into the basement, giving Dr. Umanita's dusty furniture an eerie look! More of the same chairs could be found gleaming in this dim light with a beautiful gloss in other rooms. Several other chairs were scattered throughout the other rooms. The beautiful glossy polish on the chairs and their manufacturer's logo engraved with Gothic letters on the sides indicated that they belonged to the same forbidden collection. As the lawyer said, the basement was connected to another lower floor by a wide staircase. This staircase was not much different from the staircase that connected the basement of the first floor and the ground floor. The only difference was that there was no more outside-light coming in, and pure darkness reigned everywhere.

Renzo, who was moving ahead as usual, bravely walked through the darkness and looked for the light switch with his hand. His hand slipped several times on spider webs that were piled up everywhere, and he cursed under his breath. He finally managed to find the switch. As the lights were turned on, everyone got a more accurate image of their surroundings. The basement of the second floor was different from the upper floor in several ways. First, its walls were made of stone, and its rooms were much larger. It seemed that most of the walls were removed, and only a few walls were left to divide the space on this floor. It was as if they had built a torture chamber! The lighting of the basement included a few lamps in the corners that did not have bright light. A significant number of these lamps were broken, and for this reason, the second basement was semi-dark. Here, too, they found the same things they saw upstairs—a large number of exquisite objects, which were carelessly piled up in every corner. Large porcelain vases under the flickering light and the sparkle of large, decorative metal objects in the corners gave a mysterious look to the basement. The environment was so majestic and mysterious that no one could say a word. They walked very close to each other as if they were all frightened. They felt that a terrible and dangerous animal was lurking in the darkness of this basement and was ready to attack them. Among them was only Emma, who said softly as she passed a few chairs, "These chairs are here too!" As they moved further, they came across a huge pile of large rugs spread out and stack on top of each other. It was so many of them that they would reach a person's waist height.

"Wow! look how many rugs are here!" said Ercole. As if saying this sentence had broken the spell of the space, everyone suddenly started talking,

"These are expensive, aren't they?!" said Emma nervously.

Ercole looked at the carpets expertly and said, "In this light, it is not possible to price correctly, but it is clear that the carpets are expensive!"

Frightened by the conversation, Karmelo broke away from the others and got lost in a hallway made up of several large, giant shelves. The others dared themselves and scattered around. After digging through the boxes, Amelia called out to Gino,

"Gino! Gino! Come here! there are some things here you might like!"

Gino walked over and was thrilled to see several boxes filled with phonograph records. Amelia found a gramophone in another corner of the room. In the other corner, Gino caught sight of another antique gramophone with a bronze horn. The objects in this second basement were in many ways more precious than the upper floor, and it was strange that there were unexpected objects among them. Amelia found a large German flashlight inside the treasures. No one expected the batteries in them to work since they were probably sitting there for years.

However, when Amelia pressed the key on one of them, a glowing cascade of light came out of it, and everyone gathered around this new light source in surprise. Karmelo picked up one of the flashlights and continued his tour, describing German industry and civilization. Emma's discovery encouraged others to look for a source of light. Gino soon found a lantern. Miraculously, its tank was full of oil. He lit it with a match he took from Ercole. Renzo also found an old flashlight with a metal body in a corner. The rest got their share when Renzo found a box full of colorful lanterns. It was not long before they searched the basement, each with a light in hand. Such a light source was necessary to inspect the basement because sheer darkness prevailed in many places. Someone's foot could get stuck in a box or another object

31

left on the ground and fall. Gino concluded that there was no other basement underneath this one. He wandered around the stone walls of the basement and found no way to enter a lower floor. Then, just as he was convinced that another lower floor was imaginary, his eyes caught a dark hole in the corner of a wall. He wondered if that was the entrance to another basement! He went there and saw that it was an opening to an iron door. Large yellow carnations of gold decorated the door, with heavy rings hung from the door instead of handles.

The door was apparently very old. Gino grabbed the ring and pulled it toward himself, but the door would not open. Suddenly, Gino thought of finding a lever and opening the door with it. The door opened with such a loud sound that it caught everyone's attention. Emma shouted from the other side of the basement,

"Oh my God! What was that sound?!"

The door opened easily, despite the screaming and scratching sound. Gino looked inside and saw a dreadful, vague shadow in the dark basement. Under the light of the lantern, they could see the dark hole behind the door and a few wet steps that seemed to lead to a long staircase that went down into the heart of the earth. Despite trying, Gino could not bring himself to go down the stairs alone. So, he shouted,

"My people! Come and see what I found! There is another floor below us!"

Renzo replied from somewhere nearby, "No! You must be joking!"

Renzo was relatively close and reached Gino after a few minutes. Without saying a word, he looked down the stairs through the light of his flashlight and shook his head thoughtfully. In less than five minutes, all six people gathered around the stairs leading to the third basement.

"I don't think that staircase is leading to any important place," said Ercole, after carefully looking down several times, "Maybe a small space for storing food and things that people used in the past when they didn't have electricity. In our village, the villagers used to make a hole in their yard to keep their food there during the winter."

"I do not think so," said Gino, "Those stairs have to lead to a bigger place. There is enough space on this floor to put many things. I don't think they built such a big space to store food."

Amelia also inspected the stairs and said, "Yes, the stairs are stone, the corridor is vast, there must be another floor below us."

Renzo took a deep breath and said, "Well, what are we waiting for? Let's go and see!"

Emma coughed and said, "You know, I think I'd better stay up here. It is getting humid, and you know I have asthma. I'm afraid moisture and dust would make my breathing very difficult."

Ercole immediately welcomed it, "Yes, yes, I agree with Emma. Also, Dr. Umanita said not to wander in the basement. His soul may be upset that we are doing this."

Gino's lantern light reflected Ercole's face from below, and it made his face look devilish.

"Do you believe in ghosts?!" said Renzo, sarcastically, and laughed.

"His soul?! No! He commanded us to leave the furniture here, which we are going to take with us! Then walking around means nothing!" said Amelia.

"Anyway, I can't leave Emma here alone," said Ercole.

Emma frowned at Ercole and said, "Excuse me?! I'm not a child! I would like to go back to the basement on the first floor, and I do not want help."

"Good idea! I'll come too!" said Ercole, without hesitation.

Karmelo looked at the two hesitantly and said, "But I think there are other interesting things down there! In old houses, treasures are usually hidden on the ground floor! I'd rather go down and see."

"I will go with you!" Said Amelia.

Emma handed the bigger flashlight to Amelia and said, "Take this. It is brighter than the one you have now. I'm going upstairs to the first basement to look at the sculptures for a while, and there is enough light there."

Then, the group was divided into two. Emma and Ercole looked for the staircase leading upstairs and went up. On the other hand, Gino, Renzo, Karmelo, and Amelia decided to go down the narrow staircase. As Amelia noticed, the stairs were paved with white stone, but the passage of time had changed its color. A thick layer of dust accumulated over the years combined with the basement's high humidity made a layer of slimy mud all over the basement. In some places, moss had covered the stairs, which seemed strange in the absence of light. The stairs went down in a narrow, spiral tunnel. They were slippery, and Gino's foot slipped on them once or twice. It took them a while, but they finally ended up in front of another iron door that looked like an old entrance door. Large yellow carnations of gold were on it, and a heavy ring was hung on it instead of a handle. Karmelo touched the patterns on the door with his fingertips and said,

> "It's weird; it's like they put an ancient artwork in place of a door!" He then grabbed the ring on the door and opened it with a little force.

Once again, a sharp squeak came out of the door, and the door spun slowly on his heel. All four looked ahead through the light of their flashlights and lanterns.

Emma and Ercole breathed a sigh of relief when they reached the first basement and saw the soothing outside-light coming in through the half-windows near the ceiling. They both paused for a moment after entering the floor.

Then, Emma said, "Well, I want to be alone for a little while and relax a little bit."

"Okay, we can spend a little alone time!" replied Ercole.

Emma went to a room and looked for the collection of paintings and looked through them. Ercole said to himself,

> "There are twelve large closets in that back room, all full of clothes. Maybe I find something in there I like."

Dusty objects filled the rooms, making the rooms look smaller than they really were. The outside-light came into the foggy space through the little windows next to the ceiling and gave the room an eerie feeling. After walking around the floor for a while, Ercole remembered Emma and wondered, "Where did she go? I saw her here last time."

Something caught Ercole's attention. It was a pearl bracelet with a jewel hanging from it. He picked it up from the floor and said, "Yeah, I saw this on Emma's hand." He went to look for Emma. He knew that Emma wanted to inspect the paintings they saw in one of the rooms. But he did not remember exactly which room.

The rest of the group that chose to go down to the third basement hesitated for a moment as they entered the basement. In front of them was a huge space, immersed in darkness. "Yes! Another floor!" said Karmelo triumphantly. He laughed happily, and it was echoed in the darkness of the basement. It was as if an army of goblins were laughing. They got scared and crouched together in fear. Renzo was scared by the echo of Karmelo's laughter, but he mustered up his last drop of courage and stepped in. The floor was covered with dark cobblestones, the color of which turned dark red under the flickering light of the lanterns. Karmelo swallowed his laughter and turned on his powerful flashlight. Everyone saw that the basement's high ceiling was empty of any cable, wire, and lamp.

"There's no electric light switch," whispering Renzo, searching the walls, "We have to continue with the same lights."

They all went further. This time, no trace of their past courage was left, and they wanted to stay together.

Renzo said, "We better stay together because if one of our flashlights stops working, we may get lost in the darkness."

"Okay!" whispered Amelia, but her voice echoed in the darkness of the basement. Despite its terrifying appearance, its damp, spider-infested, moldy stone walls, and its astonishing breadth, the third basement was similar to the upper floors in many ways. There were several different objects around each corner as if no one had touched them for centuries. A thick layer of dust covered everything. Everyone expected to see very old and ancient objects there. However, Amelia's flashlight soon shined on something no one expected. Karmelo froze in front of a table with an object on it for a moment and then laughed out loud! His laughter echoed in the darkness. Renzo said violently,

"Enough! shut up!" But Karmelo laughed and laughed until even he got scared of the echo of his laughter! It was clear that his laughter also stemmed from fear.

"What's so funny about that mirror?" Amelia said judgmentally.

"Can't you see?!" Said Karmelo, "It's a computer! I think it's one of those expensive computers!"

"Well, okay, so what?" Said Renzo.

"A computer!" Karmelo said, "What is a computer doing down here?! You know, I mean, someone was here recently."

Renzo pushed him and, with his flashlight pointed forward like a sword, continued his way. He muttered, "Of course someone was here recently! It is as if you have forgotten that the owner has been dead for just a month!"

"He means that it is as if no one has set foot here for centuries, but then there is a new computer here too!" said Gino.

Karmelo followed Renzo and said, "Something like this in here? But it doesn't matter. It turns out Dr. Umanita was recently here. Although, there are no footprints on the floor!"

They all looked through the basement and inspected the objects in the corners. No walls were separating the rooms, and the entire basement, with its vast area, was an open, unified space. Here, too, a huge collection of various unrelated objects piled up on the floor. There were large tables filled with colorful crystal ornaments. There was a new sport motorcycle under a cloth cover in one corner, and huge sculptures depicting strange imaginary animals could be seen in the corners. The first time Amelia caught sight of one of them, she thought she had indeed encountered a living animal and screamed. But when the others lined up around the statue and inspected it more closely, they found a huge stone statue made of azure, showing a large dragon howling. In addition to these objects, other things were thrown in the corners too: A pile of colorful, seemingly dirty clothes piled up under a metal shelf; a complete collection of eighty-three African, Thai, and Chinese masks hanging

36

from the ceiling; an old washing machine with an unknown complicated mechanical device on it; two large trunks full of colorful oyster shells and fossils of ancient animals arranged in random order; a large and stylish piano with a few inches of dirt on its; and lots of boxes full of decorative metal objects, some of which were unknown. Karmelo spent a lot of time on top of those boxes, hoping to find gold coins inside. But all he got was engraved plates, and rings and tubes, and a shiny, beautiful spiral-shaped object made of gold that resembled abstract sculptures.

The four unknowingly and gradually scattered around the third basement and looked through the various objects. Meanwhile, in the first basement, Emma watched the paintings in the room and suddenly saw one of the same chairs that were forbidden to sit on. Emma looked at the chair with fascination! She knew exactly what she had to do. But she debated whether to do it then or find a better time. There was no doubt that she would become the most creative painter in Italy by performing this ceremony. She reached out and touched the chair with her eager fingers. Behind her, next to the wall, the paintings were piled up side by side. Emma did not even look at them because she thought she found a much greater source of inspiration. She knelt by the chair and ran her fingers over the seams on its sides. She felt a movement under her fingers. It felt as if something lived inside the chair. She moved her head closer to the wooden surface and gently kissed the handle of the chair! Then, she noticed another movement, and her eyes got fixed on the chair. She was shocked! A pair of large, beautiful brown eyes, with long eyelashes, were opened in front of her on the dark chair! The eyes looked at her with intelligence and charm! It felt like it was a dream! Emma stroked the lower part of the eye with her fingertips. But the eyes suddenly disappeared.

Emma felt disappointed that she felt nothing but the smooth surface of the chair under her fingers. But what closed the eyes was not the touch of her fingers; a sound of footsteps from behind her was the cause. Someone was approaching. Emma turned and saw Ercole standing on the doorstep with embarrassment.

"What?" She asked a little angrily, "What do you want?"

Ercole blushed and said, "I'm sorry to bother you. I was looking for the restroom!"

"Well, you see, it's not here!" said Emma.

Ercole dared himself and entered the room. He looked indifferently at the chair and said, "I want to tell you a secret, Emma. Of course, I hope it stays between us!"

"What is the secret?" asked Emma.

"I have a major crush on you!" said Ercole in a childish tone.

"Well, yeah, so what?" replied Emma carelessly.

"You mean you knew?!" asked Ercole.

"Of course, it was so obvious!" said Emma.

"Seriously? so you knew!" said Ercole.

"Technically, you are just physically attracted to me, aren't you?!" Asked Emma.

"No, I really like you!" replied Ercole.

"Then prove it to me!" said Emma.

"And how do you want me to prove it to you?" asked Ercole.

"Give me half of your share of the heritage! Would you do that?!" Emma said rudely and almost like a bully.

"Of course I won't! I just said I like you! I'm not crazy!" said Ercole.

"That's what I figured!" said Emma.

"Okay, let's have fun! That's what I'm asking! In return, whenever we are voting on something, I support your side of the story! Darling, it means most of the treasure you see her!" said Ercole.

"I need more for that!" exclaimed Emma, but she wanted to have a relationship with him to use his position and make him vote to her advantage.

Emma said in a provocative tone, "Seat on the chair for me! Let me see how brave and committed you are!"

"Is that all?" asked Ercole.

"Yeah, and you cannot tell anybody about us!" replied Emma.

"Definitely!" said Ercole, happily.

Then, he sat on the chair and exclaimed, "See, it is a normal chair! They might be special in a sentimental way, but they are just chairs. You see?!"

He got up from the chair. Emma said in a seductive tone, "go to the next room and get ready. There is a bed; wait for me there, and don't come back until I come to you!"

Ercole hesitated a little bit and left the room. He went to the next room and waited for Emma. After he left, Emma turned and looked through the paintings until his footsteps could not be heard anymore.

Then, she went to the chair again. Although she was annoyed by Ercole, she got a brilliant idea after talking to him. She stood in front of the chair, bent down, kissed the chair, and sat on it. In doing so, she thought the cursed chair would treat her differently.

Chapter 4

The group in the third basement found a huge library. The library's name was unfair to what was there unless it literally meant a house full of books. The library was, in fact, a long and narrow corridor, with huge and majestic shelves. These shelves were heavy wooden bookshelves that went up to the ceiling and stacked with various books. The shelves were covered with glass doors, so there wasn't much dirt inside. Their flashlights shed light on the narrow shelves and corridors between them. Gino and Renzo were thrilled to see this huge collection of books and jumped up and down like children! Amelia was thrilled to see so many books too! The library covered an unknown area. Rows of parallel corridors between the shelves and long corridors between them continued to an unknown distance. There were so many books that the fourth-floor library resembled a small, personal collection of hand-picked texts in comparison!

"I can't believe my eyes!" said Renzo, excitedly, "It is even larger than the library of the Moscow University! You know I studied there too!"

Amelia opened one of the glass shelves and pulled out a book. There was a little dust on the book. Amelia looked at it and said,

"It is in German. Hey! look! It was published in 2005!"

Hearing this, everyone gathered around her and looked at the book in surprise. Gino scrutinized the contents of another shelf, and after pulling out a few books halfway and looking at them under a lantern light, he pulled one out. Then he hurriedly looked at its front page and said in astonishment,

"I can't believe this! this one was published three months ago!"

Karmelo scratched his head and said, "What do you mean? You wanna say this eighty-year-old relative of ours used to come all the way down here and put books on these shelves just a few months ago?"

"But if these libraries were being used, then why is there dust everywhere? Why there is there no electricity here?" asked Amelia.

"Maybe they just put a random year on the books. Don't take it seriously!" said Karmelo, who showed little interest in books. Renzo turned to him with a serious face and showed him the book in his hand, and said,

"Look at this! Look at the topic! This is a book about artificial neural networks! This is a topic that doesn't go back many decades! It is also clear from its cover that it is new!"

Karmelo said with a little concern, "Well, then the only explanation is that there is magic here! Well, what do you think? do you agree?!"

Renzo walked between the shelves with a flashlight in his hand and said,

"Don't be silly!"

Despite the basement's terrifying darkness and the damp smell that pervaded everywhere, the library was tempting for Dr. Umanita's heirs. Everyone dug through the shelves for a long time. Until Renzo and Karmelo got tired and separated from the others and circulated in other parts of the basement. Gino was looking at the books so enthusiastically that he didn't notice he was separated from the others. He hurried through the library's endless corridors, glancing at the shelves. Renzo and Amelia also walked in parallel paths with him. They, too, had forgotten the fear of the vast basement because of the interesting books. All kinds of books were there, from complex science and fiction books to folklore love stories and science fiction stories with colorful cardboard covers. Like the rest of the objects found in the basement, there was no order in the books. Antique books that were handwritten a hundred years ago were placed next to new and clean academic books that had only been out of print for a few years: Pocketbooks, exquisite leather-bound books and paintings and color photographs, ancient manuscripts with yellow pages that could be torn with a gentle touch, and large and heavy dictionaries that had to be placed on a large table first for someone to be able to open them and go through them. All of this was in the middle of a mess: A collection of comic magazines, old-fashioned periodicals, large-volume or single-issue magazines, colored comics magazines, and small booklets with legible handwriting. It would take several years to review all of these books!

The group was drowned in the books, and it caused a heavy silence in the basement. In the beginning, Renzo and Karmelo talked to each other in a quiet, whispering voice. The silence in the basement was so heavy that those whispers sounded like a loud conversation, reassuring the rest of the group that everyone's close by. But that whisper gradually ceased and was replaced by a heavy silence that was broken only by the sound of their rapid breathing in the damp, cold air and Renzo's occasional sneezing. That was all, small circles of light created by the flickering flames of lanterns or the dim light of the flashlights and the silence that filled the darkness.

Suddenly, the silence was broken by a loud shout. Everyone in the basement jumped. It was Gino's voice, who was screaming with all his might! Renzo, Amelia, and Karmelo were suddenly confronted with the horrible fact that they were all alone in the darkness! Each of them was in the middle of a hallway full of bookshelves, and they could see only a small circle around themselves in the dim light of their flashlight or lantern. There were no signs of others. They could still hear Gino scream. It sounded to be out of fear.

"Do not be afraid, Gino! I'm coming your way!"

shouted Renzo and started running in Gino's direction. After a couple of minutes, he reached a crossroad between the bookshelves. For a moment, Gino saw Renzo's flashlight moving in another direction.

"Renzo, I'm here!" he shouted with hope! The flashlight stopped, turned towards him, then Gino heard Renzo's footsteps. On the other side, Karmelo's voice rose, screaming in a frightened voice, saying, "What happened? What happened? Did a snake bit someone?!"

Karmelo and Amelia ran in the direction of the other two. As they walked out of the hallway, they saw Gino's flashlight on the floor. Renzo's foot got stuck in a box full of china in the middle of the trail and fell to the ground. The dishes broke, and Renzo fell to the ground. But with an agility that was unlike him, he got up and kept moving.

Emma left the room where she spent some intimate time with Ercole in the first basement in the upper basement. She wandered around a few rooms and returned to the same room where the paintings were located. Suddenly, she felt tired, and the sleepless night took its toll on her. Her eyes were burning, and her eyelids were heavy. The basement's space with the yard light coming in through the window created a sleepy atmosphere. She wondered why the others hadn't returned from the basements below. But she was too tired to be able to focus on them. Unconsciously, she went to the chair and bent to sit on it without thinking. But she saw something that made her pause. She hesitantly touched what she saw. It was a large and silver ring with a skull engraved on it. She saw it on Renzo's finger the other day, and now she saw it on a chair.

She reached to pick it up but was surprised to find out that the ring was stuck in the chair! There was a little swelling on the surface of the chair where the ring was stuck. Emma's fingers were drawn on the chair's surface, which was now strangely transparent, but she could not touch the ring stuck in it. The ring was clearly visible, though. Emma looked at Renzo's ring in surprise and said, "How could it be stuck in the chair?" Suddenly, she heard an unfamiliar voice telling her to sit on the chair to become powerful. Emma looked around in surprise and asked, "Who is this?" She didn't hear any answer. Emma thought that perhaps anyone who sits on this chair owns all this inheritance and suddenly remembered that she forced Ercole to sit on it! After all, didn't Ercole achieve his dream, which was having Emma in his arms and making love to her? She cursed herself for making Ercole the owner of everything, even herself! Then, she thought she was the only one who saw the chair's eyes, so perhaps the chair likes her more than the others! She decided to sit on the chair and reclaim all that she had lost. She immediately sat on it. But to her surprise, she felt that her body was burning. She couldn't bear it anymore, so she got up from the chair and began to examine the chair. When she bent down and looked under the chair, she saw a white spot protruding from the middle of the lower part of the chair.

She reached for it, touched the corner, and picked it up. It was a white paper with 'Sentenced to Death' written on it! It was not clear why or who put it under the chair.

Emma got up in a panic and walked away from the chair. Suddenly, she felt threatened. She was terrified that she was left alone in that room with one of those chairs. She felt Dr. Umanita's spirit was wandering in that house, and it was going to destroy them all, one by one! She thought to herself that she must get out of this cursed basement as soon as possible. She went to the door. She heard Ercole's voice came from far away but did not intend to tell him. She preferred just to inform

43

the others and go upstairs as soon as possible! If she left alone, it was possible that others would make bad decisions in her absence. If she told Ercole that she wanted to leave, he would want to go with her and would keep harassing her. So, she moved toward the direction that the others went and called aloud, "Amelia! Gino! Renzo! Karmelo! where are you?"

When Renzo and Karmelo saw Amelia, they felt a little embarrassed because they forgot about her and left her alone among the shelves! Renzo and Karmelo found Gino and rushed to him. A few steps away, a dark chair shined under the lanterns. Not a speck of dust could be seen on it. Renzo leaned over Gino and asked,

"Gino, what happened? What happened?"

Gino had his eyes closed and held his head in his hands. He seemed unharmed but deeply disturbed!

"He's fine!" Karmelo said with a sigh of relief, "I thought maybe he got bitten by a snake or something, but he is okay!"

Using his flashlight, Renzo glanced around suspiciously. But the dim light did not show much in their radius. It was just a dark chair sitting there and looked like a mirage in the middle of the night. Renzo turned and said,

"Gino, look at me! What happened?"

Gino was breathing heavily, and his face was drenched in sweat. His clothes were wet too, and he looked terrified. This seemed odd for a person like him, who was not afraid of anything and was first to volunteer to enter dark and scary places.

"I saw its eyes, its eyes!" Gino said under his breath.

Amelia gently took his hand and said, "Calm down, Gino! We are all here with you! Nothing happened! Tell me whose eyes you saw?"

"I saw the chair's eyes, the chair's eyes!" Gino said with trembling lips, "I saw it with my eyes!"

"Chair? What chair?" asked Karmelo.

"I think he is talking about the chairs we saw on the upper floors. I only saw one or two of them on this floor," replied Amelia.

Renzo leaned over Gino again and said, "Gino, tell us what you saw! What do you mean by eyes? Whose eyes did you see?"

Gino stood up with a little effort and leaned on his friends' arms. His knees were still shaking. He complained in a trembling voice, "You won't believe me; you'll think I'm crazy!"

"No, I believe you! Tell me what you saw!" said Renzo, seriously.

"Chair, this dark chair, the ones we were told not to sit on. Now I understand why the doctor put this condition in his will!" said Gino.

"Well, why? Did you sit on it?" Amelia asked, Excited.

Gino wiped the sweat from his forehead with his wrinkled sleeves. Then, he collected himself and said,

"Well, I know you will not believe a word I say, but I'll say it. When we were searching here, Karmelo saw a tray full of coins and was distracted."

Suddenly, Karmelo said with indescribable joy, "Oh yeah! There is a huge tray full of old gold coins; you won't believe it!"

Renzo frowned at Karmelo to quiet him and asked kindly, "Well, what happened next, Gino?"

"Nothing," said Gino, "I don't know much about coins and things like that, so I went and looked elsewhere. At first, I noticed the glass cupboard and the Greek mythological sculptures, especially one that was made of transparent red crystal, caught my eye. I went to open the glass door to look at it, and suddenly, I saw this dark chair,"

Gino pointed to the chair with trembling fingers. Everyone looked at him with eyes full of anticipation until he continued,

"After that, I felt I really wanted to go and sit in that chair. I honestly think I heard a voice too, telling me to go sit in it! It sounded like my previous lover. It said it knew I was tired, and it was time for me to rest a bit!"

Karmelo said in disbelief, "You are delusional! I did not hear a sound!"

Gino continued, "I do not know what happened that I felt so exhausted. I felt that sitting in that chair was the best thing I could do. My mind went blank as if I had a cold and could not think of anything but fire and heat! As I heard that sound, I involuntarily went to the chair and sat in it!"

"Well, what happened? How was it?" asked Amelia hurriedly.

"Suddenly, I saw the reflection of my flashlight in that red statue, and I came back to consciousness," Gino said, "It was scorching! I do not know what happened, but I felt afraid of that chair. I immediately jumped up and felt there was something dangerous in it. I felt there was a great danger. But I still thought I had to go back and sit down. It was like a strong temptation that I don't know why I couldn't shake off. To distract me, I turned my back on the chair and decided to walk away. Just as I was turning around, I saw a movement on the surface of the chair. It was as if something like a beetle or a mouse was moving on its dark and smooth surface!"

"What was it?" Said Karmelo with a little concern, "Wasn't it a snake?!"

"No! What snake?! Quit talking about snakes!" Gino said, "When I saw that movement, I turned back and faced the chair and saw..." Gino paused for a moment, "I saw..."

"You are killing us! What did you see when you turned back?!" Exclaimed Renzo.

"I saw that the chair was looking at me!" said Gino, "It had a pair of eyes! A pair of real eyes. It was as if a piece of a person's face was engraved on it. But those eyes were authentic: A pair of eyes with eyebrows and eyelashes and eyelids and everything. It was looking at me. It had a look in those eyes as if it hated me or was angry! The chair's eyes were staring straight at me. I saw them myself. A pair of eyes, on a chair!"

Gino said this and calmed down a bit. Everyone was silent and looked at him in astonishment! Karmelo, standing behind Gino with Gino leaning on his arm, made a face and tapped his forehead with his free hand, meaning that Gino's lost his faculties! The first person to break the silence was Renzo. He asked,

"Look, Gino, tell me one more time to make sure if I understood correctly. You said there was a pair of eyes on the chair? You mean, like, a pair of eyeballs? As if it came out of a hole? Something like that fell on a chair?"

"No! No! It wasn't like that at all!" Gino said in a louder voice than usual, "It was a pair of eyes, like my eyes and yours. As our eyes are fixed on our faces, so were those eyes on the chair. It was as if the chair had a face and a pair of eyes on it! It was so scary, just like an animal's eyes, full of anger and viciousness! Clearly, when it closes its eyelids, we can't see them anymore. Because we don't see them now!"

"So, you are saying the chair in front of us has a pair of eyes?!" Renzo said in a tone of disbelief, "Eyes like ours?!"

"I knew you wouldn't believe me!" said Gino, "But it's the truth! This is what I saw! This chair has eyes!" He stayed silent for a while and grabbed his head with his hands again and said, "I do not know! It looks like I've lost my mind! Maybe I have?"

"Look, cousin," said Karmelo, firmly, "If you think you saw the eyes on that chair, you definitely imagined it. There is no doubt! And don't think you are a fool or anything. We all see weird things in the dark."

"Maybe there's a hole in that chair, and it looked like a pair of eyes under the reflection of your flashlight," said Renzo.

With that said, Karmelo moved toward the chair. The chair, just like an innocent, lifeless body of wood, stood in front of him, gleaming under the light of their lanterns and flashlights with its fine, dark wood. He pointed to the side Gino showed them and said,

"There is no trace of a hole here," Then he pressed the palm of his hand against the wood and said, "Strange! It is so hot! as if it was not sitting in a cold basement like this! Gino! are you sure you weren't sitting in it for a while? Maybe when you sat down, you fell asleep and had a dream."

Gino regained control and tried to say something sensible, "I just sat on it for a short time."

Like the rest of the basement, the floor around the chair was covered in dust and dirt, leaving only traces of Gino and Karmelo's footprints.

"How cool these are!" Karmelo said, "I like these chairs! They look very comfortable! Let's all sit in them!"

Renzo stepped forward and stood shoulder to shoulder with Karmelo, looked pessimistically at the chair, and said,

"No, why should we sit in it?" He hit his fist to where the eyes should've been. Renzo said triumphantly, "Do you see? There are no eyes!"

For a moment, Karmelo felt the chair trembled under his hands. But this moment passed quickly. Amelia stood next to them and said provocatively,

"What happened? Are you afraid, Renzo ?!"

"No, why should I be afraid of a piece of wood?! Let me try and sit first!" said Renzo, embarrassed.

Then, he sat down in the chair, and after a while, he felt an intense heat, but he did not say anything so he wouldn't scare the others. Karmelo and Amelia took turns and sat in it. They were all eager to see what it felt like to sit in one of those chairs. They felt the same warmth one by one, but for the same reason, they did not say anything to others. Then, Gino tried to smile,

"I think I've become delusional! But what happened that made me so scared? Why was the chair so hot?"

"I think we're all exhausted," said Renzo to change the subject, "That is why we imagine things like this. Anyway, we've been up since last night, and we've been going around these basements. Let's go upstairs and rest a little bit."

"I agree," said Karmelo, "Emma and Ercole must be well-rested by now!"

"But we have not seen the lowest floor yet," said Amelia, "We were going to go down to see how many floors there are."

"You mean you think there's a floor below this basement? I do not think so!" said Karmelo while rolling his eyes.

"Why not? There was a hole in the floor with a row of narrow stairs at the bottom of the hallway between the bookshelves. I'm sure there is another floor below us!" insisted Amelia.

"That one must be a treasure trove!" said Karmelo.

The echo of his voice reminded everyone of the horror of the first minutes they entered this floor. They also heard a similar statement from him at that time. But now, there was something ominous in the darkness of the underground that worried everyone.

"Guys," Renzo said impatiently, "I think we stayed here long enough! It's time to go upstairs and take a break. If you want, we can come down again in a few hours and explore everywhere."

"But I'm not tired," said Karmelo, "I want to know how many basements this house has. This is the first time I see a house built to this depth in the ground!"

"I want to go down there too! I am no longer afraid of the chairs and things like that! I say now that we are here, let's go down and see there too, just a glance, and then we'll be back up soon!" said Amelia.

Renzo said sarcastically, "Let's say we found another staircase that went down again. What then?! Do you want to go down forever? Do you want to go to the other side of the earth?!"

"Don't be silly! Maybe we find one more basement, but it's not possible to find more than that!" said Gino.

"Yeah? why not?" Said Renzo, "Did you think there would be a third basement?"

49

There was silence for a moment, and then they thought of all the possibilities. Finally, Amelia made her decision and said,

"I am not superstitious, but I think there is something down here that made Dr. Umanita warn us so much in his will! That's why I don't think it's wise for us to search the basements separately. If you agree, let's go down as a group and just look around."

"Well, what if we didn't succeed?" Said Renzo, "I think before we all lose it, we should go back upstairs and take a break."

"I'm not going back up now, and as I said, I don't want to go down alone."

"Okay, I will go down with you," said Gino, "If we all went down and took a look instead of arguing, we would've been back already!"

"I don't think we should get separated," said Renzo.

"I don't know about you, but I'll go back upstairs!" said Karmelo.

"Well, what should we do?" asked Renzo undecidedly.

"It's clear, give the good lanterns to Amelia and me, and we will go check out the downstairs and will be back quickly," said Gino.

"Okay, I think there is no other way. Gino and Amelia go down to the next basement. Karmelo goes up, and I stay here. If you need help, I will come down; otherwise, you come back up, and we all will return to the first floor. How does that sound?" asked Renzo.

Gino didn't think it was a good idea for Renzo to stay alone in that basement, but everyone agreed at last. Some flashlights weren't working properly, so they changed their flashlights with Karmelo's lantern. Renzo kept the strongest flashlight because he was going to stay there alone.

Amelia couldn't remember the correct direction for the hole to the lower basement. But she remembered that the hole was at the end of one of the corridors between the library shelves. The two walked the long, dark corridors, and when they saw no sign of the hole, they returned and took another corridor. Until finally, they saw a hole in the floor. The hole had no door or other marks. It was simply a hole in the ground with a staircase going down. The stairs twisted around and turned around an axis. The surrounding walls were narrow, and Amelia and Gino could barely cross it. The two went down the stairs for a long time.

Chapter 5

The room Emma was supposed to be in was further away in the first basement than Ercole expected. Ercole entered the hallway and saw Emma calling others. Although the lights were dim, it was clear that Ercole's face turned red! A vein swelled on his forehead, and he roared at Emma, grabbed her shirt, and said,

"Where are you going?"

Emma screamed, "What are you doing? Let go of my shirt!"

"What did you do with my dagger?" shouted Ercole.

"What dagger? Are you crazy?! I did not see any dagger!" replied Emma.

"Do you think I'm a kid and you can deceive me? Keep your lies for someone else! The later you confess, the more it's going to hurt! I saw in my dream that you attacked me with my dagger!" said Ercole.

"You idiot! It was a dream! This is the reality now, not a dream!" said Emma. Then she slapped Ercole's hands away from her shirt and said with a sarcastic laugh, "Seems like what we did was so good that you lost your mind!" As she was leaving the room, she said, "Jackass!"

When they reached the narrow corridor's end, Gino and Amelia found themselves in a large open space. The ceiling of the fourth basement was extremely high. The stairs continued to descend for a relatively long distance. When they finally reached the last step, they found themselves in a large space. The light from the lanterns was not enough to see the ceiling or the walls. The dim reflections of light and bright spots could occasionally be seen on the walls. The ceiling in the distance seemed to have an uneven surface. There was no sign of the beautiful cobblestones of the upper floors down there. The ground beneath their feet was rough and rocky as if they were standing on the floor of a limestone cave. The air was humid. Amelia said in a low voice,

"I hope we don't suffocate here from the smoke of the lanterns; the air is not breathable!"

"I don't think so," Gino said softly, "Look, it's so wide here that you can breathe for a few weeks. It is not at all clear where the walls are!" They both dared to raise their lanterns and stared in amazement at the scene in front of them.

Just like the upper floors, they saw a pile of cluttered things that were thrown everywhere. The first thing that caught their eyes was a dark chair right in front of the stairs as if inviting them to rest! Suddenly, Amelia felt incredibly tired. She wanted to sit down and catch her breath. She couldn't sit on the ground; it was too uneven and damp. But that chair! There wasn't even a little bit of dust on it, and Amelia was sure it was as warm as the chairs upstairs. Amelia suddenly came to her senses when she heard Gino say in horror, "What are you doing?" He firmly grabbed Amelia's hand. Amelia blinked and saw that Gino grabbed her hand before she sat in the chair. Amelia let Gino's strong hands pull her away from the chair, and she felt sick and felt a strong headache.

"We shouldn't sit on these as a precaution," said Gino.

"Yeah, yeah, I remember; I was just a little tired!" said Amelia while regaining consciousness.

"Well, there's nothing wrong with that!" said Gino. He paused and asked, "What do you remember from sitting on the chair?"

"When I sat on the chair upstairs to help you overcome your fear, I suddenly felt my body burning from the chair's heat, but I didn't say anything so you wouldn't get scared even more!" said Amelia.

"Okay, we saw whatever we wanted to see here!" Gino said, "I don't think there is another floor below here."

"We'll go back right away," said Amelia, "Let's just take a look around."

Then, she took a few steps and looked at the things around them. The glow of what was piled up in front of them in several big boxes left them speechless. Karmelo was right! There was a treasure hidden there! Several heavy and huge boxes were placed on the ground right in front of them. Each of them was so large that two or three people could stand inside it! The brown leather strap that covered the boxes turned yellow under the lanterns' light. The doors of all the chests were half-open, and the reflection of lanterns' light on the jewels piled up inside them dazzled their eyes! Gino and Amelia stared at the boxes with amazement! Then, they both approached the boxes, placed their lanterns on the floor in a coordinated motion, and cautiously touched the boxes' contents. It was as if they were afraid this was a dream! But the piled-up boxes were still in front of them! It wasn't a dream! Amelia dipped her hand into a box and pulled out a handful of large red jewels. Then she turned to Gino, who thoughtfully held a large winged-lion in his hand and looked at it carefully.

"It's all gold, I can't believe it!" said Gino, "Do you know what wealth each piece of this is?!"

Then he carefully placed the statue back in the box and picked up his lantern, and walked to the other boxes. Inside all of them were full of exquisite jewels. Boxes seemed to be countless as their rows continued into dark, hidden corners. Gino walked away from Amelia with a lantern and walked in the dark. Then, he called her and said, "Come and see this!" Amelia picked up her lantern and followed him. Gino stood in front of a huge statue of an armored horseman. The statue was of accurate human size and showed a hero riding a horse.

Gino ran his fingers over the cold metal of the sculpture and said, "Bronze, look how natural and delicate it is!" Amelia picked up her lantern and walked a few steps ahead, a full row of seated eagles carved out of red stone lined up in front of her. It was too many of them, and she could not see the last one.

"Look at these statues," said Amelia, "There's at least fifty of them! Who made them? I think they are made of marble."

"Just the wealth that lies here is enough for all of us to live comfortably with our children and grandchildren for the rest of our lives!" said Gino.

Amelia thought for a moment and looked at him with shining eyes. It was as if she wanted to say something, but she was hesitant. Gino felt the awkwardness and said,

"What? What you want to say?" It was as if he wanted to say the same thing and hoped to hear it from someone else! Seeing Amelia's silence, he insisted,

"Tell me, what is it?"

"How important do you think it is for others to know this basement exists?!" asked Amelia, "After all, we were the only ones who dared to come down here and found these. Others still think this is a food storage hole!"

Gino felt giddy and said, "Only you and me?"

A voice from a short distance replied, "No, it is not the right thing to do!"

Amelia and Gino were startled! They looked in the direction of the sound in the darkness. They heard a burst of laughter! Then the light of Renzo's bright flashlight lit up his face! He was standing in front of them! Amelia said with a little annoyance,

"Oh, is it you, Renzo?! I thought you were upstairs!"

"Yeah, I was!" said Renzo, "I walked around on that floor for a while, but then when I saw no noise coming from upstairs, I thought Karmelo went upstairs safely. That's why I thought to come down here and make sure you were safe too!"

"You know, I did not mean that!" said Amelia in a soft tone.

Renzo interrupted, "I know exactly what you meant! If Ercole or Emma were here, they would've thought the same thing! That is, do not worry too much. Even I, when I saw this wealth, was tempted to take you out of my way! I said to myself, what is the reason for Ercole wasting one-sixth of this, or for Emma to spend this money on show off to her old neighbors and relatives? A whole lot of interesting work can be done with this money!"

"Well, I was thinking the same thing, but ..." said Gino.

"I know! But it is not right for you to do this. I disagree with depriving others of their rights. By the way, I was just looking around and all of a sudden, I found something!" said Renzo.

"What did you find?" asked Gino.

"I have to show it to you on the way back," said Renzo.

Amelia tried to make up for her words, so she said, "I take back what I said. I should not have made that offer. There is so much wealth here that all of us and many generations after us can live comfortably!"

55

"But there is a drawback. These cannot be taken out of here!" said Gino.

"Why not? We will put the jewelry in big bags and take them upstairs," said Renzo.

Gino showed him the bronze statue and said, "Yes, jewelry can be taken, but what about this statue? Or those marble eagles? They cannot be passed through this narrow corridor. Now I'm sure there are other things in this basement as well."

Amelia said with a scared tone, "But then how did they bring these here? They couldn't have been made here!"

"There must be another way out," said Renzo, "Of course, if we look, we will find such a way. Maybe that corridor next to the stairs is the key to the story. Although it was very narrow as well."

"Corridor? What corridor?" asked Amelia.

Renzo said, "Oh, didn't you see it? A corridor starts from where you entered the basement and goes down with a steep slope. But it is so narrow that these cannot be brought from there either."

"You mean, maybe there's a floor underneath this one too?! Five basements?! More than the floors of the building?!" said Gino with amazement.

"It is not unlikely!" said Renzo, thoughtfully, "Of course, this can no longer be called a basement! This is more like a cave! Do you see how far the roof is from the ground?! Maybe it was a subway tunnel or an abandoned mine."

"Okay," said Gino, "Let's see where that corridor leads to."

"You do not want to search this floor? I think there are many things around that we have not seen yet." Said Renzo.

Ercole was kneeling in front of a large couch in the central hall in the first basement, whispering incomprehensible sentences under his breath. From the moment he set foot in this basement, he felt like there was a heavy curse on this house and all the treasures hidden in it. Maybe it was because Dr. Umanita was not happy with them usurping his property in the basements.

Emma was standing in the room that contained the painting and was anxiously waiting for the others to return. She was looking at the dark chair. She was worried that the ones that went downstairs might be dead already! She was thinking, why these things happened to them? What if only she and Ercole had survived? She was thinking about how that paper was put under this chair. Could it be that Ercole intentionally put the paper when he sat on the chair? Is he a direct threat, and should she beware?

Ercole found his dagger and was thinking to himself on the other side of the hall. Suddenly, he heard a voice that said this whole thing had nothing to do with Dr. Umanita's curse. He had to take Dr. Umanita's heirs, one by one, and take all the inheritance! Because from the beginning, their names were entered into the will by mistake. They are not the real heirs, only he is! The chairs understood this! They recognized the real heir of this house! Ercole! That's why he heard that voice! It sounded like the voice of one of his school teachers. That voice encouraged him to destroy others. Among them all, only he, Ercole Umanita, could neutralize the effect of this curse.

Only he knew how to tame the evil spirit in the chairs. Now, he was kneeling in front of the chair, whispering the spells in a low tone. He was sure he had to satisfy the chairs in some way! He must show them that he loves them, that he is useful to them, and will sincerely serve them! He had to show them his servitude and humility! He thought it was only under this condition that they would allow him to return to earth once more and see the light of day as the sole heir of this great house. Ercole looked out the small window near the ceiling. Despite the dirty glass, night stars could be seen. The basement light was very dim. It was only when it got dark that they realized how insufficient the lights in the rooms were. Such a large area, about a thousand square yards. He calculated the number of lamps he would need to light up the building. Next, he thought of a house with a thousand yards of infrastructure. The house that belonged only to him, from tomorrow morning! Of course, he would have trouble explaining what happened to the other heirs. But everyone would be buried until then. He is the only one that's left—he who knew how to cope with the chairs and satisfy them! Dr. Umanita's house and the surrounding gardens were a gift from these large, powerful chairs! Now, looking closer, he realized that the whole story resembled a predetermined plot: Dr. Umanita's will, his coming to this house, and how he felt from the beginning that the rest of the heirs were irrelevant people and that this house should legally belong only to him! Years ago, during the heyday of the Italian mafia, Ercole tried to persuade his colleagues to confiscate Dr. Umanita's property to collaborate with the mafia and establish himself as a full-fledged police informant.

But Dr. Umanita did not agree to sign the papers. Although the older man was ill in those days, he resisted Ercole's pressures. Dr. Umanita was not guilty of anything, so he couldn't be kept in jail for more than a day or two. He was not involved in economic crimes, nor did he have any quarrels or dark financial books that Ercole could use against him. That's why they couldn't hold him in jail. From that day on, he kept waiting for Dr. Umanita to die. He thought Dr. Umanita would die in a year or two. Then, since Dr. Umanita had no children and no close relative, he could go there under the pretext of inspecting the place and leave a fake will there, which would introduce Ercole as Dr. Umanita's heir! But this time, too, the older man had the upper hand! Ercole felt an old, blind rage sprouting in his heart. He would always be angry if he were tricked. The older man had deceived him this time as well, and he survived twenty-five years after the day he had spent in jail and left a valid will to his lawyer. Ercole could not believe that after everything he'd done to the older man, he would mention Ercole's name as one of the heirs. He felt like he liked the late doctor for a short time and recited a prayer for the forgiveness of his soul! But then he felt everything was so unfair! The other heirs did not even know Dr. Umanita! Only Ercole knew the doctor before he died. So, he should be the only heir!

He knew that the others who claimed to know Dr. Umanita were lying. He was the closest one to him. He was the one who spent many days in this house as a child when his mother and father were working in this house. Until his father got a new job and never went back to see the doctor again. However, he changed his name to Umanita to show his devotion to the doctor. Ercole had worked very hard to take possession of this house. He was the one who interrogated the doctor and talked to him every day for a month so that he could confess to him and confiscate his property for his links to the mafia. It was not fair for others to inherit anything. They all had to step aside in his favor, and now these were the powerful and magical chairs that were going to make his dream come true! He realized this the moment he saw the chairs. They cursed everyone but him, leaving the house to him, the only true heir of Dr. Umanita! But to keep the chairs satisfied, he had to make a sacrifice. He had to prove his sincerity to them. He had to make an effort for the chairs to realize his devotion to them. That is why he had to do this. A moan tore his thoughts. Emma opened her eyelids with great difficulty and looked at Ercole with frightened eyes. Ercole avoided looking at her. He knew he did not need to look at her. He did not even have to worry about her reaction because she did not understand anything. She did not understand the greatness of this story. This was her inevitable fate. She had to be a victim.

That was why she was now lying on the cold ground with her hands and feet tied like a lifeless body next to his feet, right next to the same paintings that she enjoyed so much. He bent down and arranged Emma's messy, blood-stained hair. He remembered that he instinctively attacked Emma with a dagger. Then, he picked her up and threw her on the chair. He felt that the other heirs had entered his territory and that he had to destroy them all. Emma made noises and pointed at him with her eyes. Ercole carefully positioned her on the chair, rested her head on her hands, and stretched her legs so that her body had the highest level of contact with the dark wooden chair. He whispered in Emma's ear,

"Emma, I have to do this! I know you do not understand, but don't worry! You will understand the truth very soon! You, too, will become part of this powerful being! I promise you will have fun!"

Emma didn't hear Ercole's last words. A heavy sleep overcame her, and she lost her life. Ercole leaned back in his chair and formally offered his victim to the chair.

Chapter 6

Gino moved downstairs, and the others followed. Renzo guessed it was likely that they would stay down there for a long time, so he turned his flashlight off and followed the others. Clinging to each other, the three of them walked through the damp, sticky chaos of the basement, which smelled of antiquity. They passed through a strange collection of the most exquisite objects they had ever seen. Despite the narrow corridor leading to this floor, everything was built to a gigantic size.

It was as if those who brought those items there enjoyed the mystery of how those things were transported to the basement! There were huge porcelain vases in the corners that a big man like Renzo could easily hide inside one of them! There were many statues in the corners, some of which were made out of gold and were shining stunningly! There were all kinds of statues down there, huge crystal statues resembling Chinese monks with long robes, azure and dark stone statues depicting soldiers from different periods of the world's history, and several lions, leopards, deer, and snake statues were made of white marble and looked life-like. From time to time, they came across huge boxes full of marvelous things. One box was full of Roman gold coins, and the other was full of pearls. The view there was like the treasury of a Thousand-and-One-Night Palace. The difference was that from time to time, among these exquisite objects, one of those dark chairs appeared like an awkward scene in the middle of an eye-catching view. Finally, after a little wandering and without any discussion, they moved to the stairs that they used to get down there. There, Renzo showed them a narrow corridor they didn't see before. The corridor, as Renzo described, was very narrow and sloped downhill. It was shorter than it seemed initially and soon led to a small room with stone walls with nothing but a dark chair.

The room had several doors. Amelia separated from them to go to one of the other rooms to use as a restroom. Gino, feeling that his thirst was getting unbearable, waited for Amelia to come back to suggest to everyone to go back upstairs. He wandered around the room to pass the time. The whole hall was full of strange objects. Dirty maps written in strange handwriting were hung on doors and walls, and many dried animals were placed on narrow, dark tables. As Gino walked around, he walked into one of the half-opened doors and, to his amazement, saw a staircase adorned with delicate silver railings going down. There was another dark chair next to him. Suddenly, the sound of footsteps rose from behind him. He turned and said with hope, "Amelia?" But saw the light of Renzo's flashlight approaching him from a distance and realized he was wrong. Renzo excitedly showed him what he had in his hand. It was a small clay plate with holes in it. Renzo said,

"Do you see this? It is an inscription!"

Gino grabbed it in disbelief, examining the dimples under the lantern. They seemed to have written things in italics. He said in surprise, "Where did you find this?!"

"There's a big library full of these in that room across the room we were in," said Renzo, "They are arranged very neatly on wooden shelves. They are likely to be old."

"Old inscriptions can't be so intact!" said Gino.

After his thought, he laughed and said, "Unless they have been here since day one!" At that moment, Renzo suddenly looked around and asked, "Wait a minute, where is Amelia?"

"She went to that room; she went to the restroom," replied Gino.

With an unusual reaction, Renzo panicked and ran to the door that Gino showed him. Gino thought that Renzo wanted to open the door for a moment, so he ran behind Gino to stop him. But Renzo stood behind the door and said loudly,

"Amelia?! Amelia?!"

Amelia's voice could be heard in the distance, whispering, "I'm here. Wait, I'm getting up now!"

Renzo raised an eyebrow at the last sentence and looked at Gino! Then, he squatted on the floor right behind the door and turned his flashlight off. Gino put his lantern on the table and sat down next to Renzo. Then, he sighed and said,

"Badly thirsty!"

"Yeah," said Renzo, "We have to go back up soon. We have all our lives to wander down here."

"There's another floor below here! I found another staircase that goes down behind that door. It has beautiful silver railings, and of course, there is a dark chair next to it!" said Gino.

Renzo frowned at the mentioning of the chair and closed his eyes. Gino noticed his discomfort and put his hand on Renzo's shoulder and said,

"I know, we made the mistake of leaving you alone in the basement upstairs. Especially after the nonsense, I said about that chair!"

Renzo opened his shiny eyes. He seemed to have a world of painful memories emanating from within. When he began to speak, his voice sounded like a whisper. He said,

"I am not afraid of the darkness and loneliness. I was imprisoned for three years in a crypt smaller than my height. In pure darkness. I almost went insane and thought I was blind, but I gradually got better after being released. I do not think anyone is as accustomed to darkness and loneliness as I am!"

Gino stared at Renzo for a moment and said, "You were a prisoner?" And when Renzo nodded in confirmation, he asked, "Where?"

Renzo shook his head again and said, "Yes, we were on a yacht with our friends when the Somali pirates attacked us and captured us and demanded ransom for our release, and then when they saw that there was no money, they released us. In general, I am a restless person. I am a lot calmer now, though." Then, as if remembering something, he got up and said, "But what made me come down was not darkness and loneliness. Even when I was upstairs, I turned off my flashlight for a while so that the battery would not run out. Until I heard my lover's voice."

Gino thought he heard it wrong, so he repeated, "Your lover's voice?!"

"Look! I am not a superstitious person! Honestly, I do not believe in anything! But there is something terrible in this house! Yes, in the dark, I heard a hissing sound, and when I turned the flashlight on, I saw another dark chair behind me!" said Renzo.

"Do you remember if the chair was there already?" asked Gino.

Renzo thought about it. As far as he could remember, there was only one chair in front of him. So, he said with a little fear,

"No! I don't remember any chair there! When I turned on the light, I saw another chair behind me too! The hissing sound came from the same direction. It was as if the chair moved towards me in the dark!"

"It can't be that way!" said Gino, "A chair does not move by itself!"

"These are not ordinary chairs!" said Renzo, "Something is in contact with them. Remember how hot it got when we sat on them? There was no dust on any of them. I think you saw something that you were so scared of. You do not look like a coward to me! Gino, did you not hear a voice up there?"

"What kind of voice?" asked Gino.

"Anything, a voice that speaks to you. Because I heard a voice, but I do not know if what she said is true or false," replied Renzo.

"What did that voice say to you?" Asked Gino.

"I cannot say," replied Renzo, "It's personal. I think that Dr. Umanita had a good reason for insisting that we shouldn't enter the basement and sit on those chairs." Renzo paused for a moment and then continued, "Honestly, when I was alone there, I had a feeling. It is as if my lover was telling me to sit on the chair! A compelling voice that sounded very much like hers. I gave in to the sound and sat down on the chair!"

Gino thought about it and said, "I heard a voice too! I have never seen so many chairs in a set. Almost everywhere we go, we see some of them. These may have something like a curse or evil spirits in them! I think I have seen forty chairs down here so far. Doesn't that sound weird?! Another weird thing is that the chairs are right where you might be tired when you get there! Remember?! one of them was down the narrow stairs.

There was another one in this next room." He pointed to the room where Amelia was!

Renzo and Gino both jumped up and looked at each other! Gino beat on the door and shouted, "Amelia? Amelia? Aren't you done? Are you okay?"

But there was no answer! No trace of her lantern light through the gap either! Gino put his hand on the door handle and shouted louder than before, "Amelia? Amelia? do you hear me?" He then pressed the handle but was surprised to find that the door was locked. Amelia did not lock the door. There was no reason for locking the door either; there was no one there but the three of them.

When Renzo saw that the door was locked, he hit it with his torso without any delay. Frightened, Gino pushed the knob up and down a few times, but the door was locked. Renzo kept hitting on the door with unbelievable strength. Eventually, Gino was convinced that this was the only way to enter the room, so he joined Renzo. Finally, after a little pushing and hitting, the wooden door broke under the weight of their shoulders and came out of its hinge. Gino dropped the door on the floor and rushed into the room. In front of them was a scene they were subconsciously waiting for. There was no sign of Amelia's lantern light in the room. At the end of the long room in front of them was a large dark chair, and the walls of the room were covered with large, incomprehensible patterns. At the end of the room, an object was detectable on the dark chair. Renzo and Gino ran to the chair.

It was Amelia who was on the chair. Her eyes were closed, and she was pale. She did not seem to be breathing. Her lantern was on the ground right next to her feet. Renzo and Gino grabbed Amelia's cold and hands and tried to lift her off the chair. For a moment, it seemed to them that Amelia's body was glued to the chair and could not be detached from it. But that feeling disappeared, and the intoxicated Amelia was placed in Gino's arms. Renzo carefully took her pulse and said,

"Her pulse is so weak!" Then, with the back of his hand, he slapped Amelia gently. Gino pushed Renzo's hand away and stabilized Amelia's loose neck in his arms. He then shouted,

"Amelia! Amelia! Wake up! Get up, girl!"

Amelia's eyelids moved a little, and she opened her eyes with great difficulty. Then, she closed her eyes again. Renzo sighed in relief as she regained consciousness. His lover's voice told him that if Amelia did not survive, he too would be destroyed and would never see the sunlight again!

Renzo and Gino waited a little while for Amelia to recover. She seemed to be much better as soon as she was lifted from that chair. Her cheeks were slowly showing normal color, and her heart rate was getting stronger. Finally, after a few anxious minutes, she opened her eyes and saw that she was in Gino's arms. She gathered herself and asked in a sleepy voice,

"What happened?!"

Gino let her stand on her feet. Then said, "We do not know! You tell us what happened! We found you in that dark chair."

Amelia looked around in confusion, and when her eyes fell on the chair, she said, "Oh, the chair, I sat on the chair, didn't I?" She asked in a loud and fearful voice.

Renzo and Gino nodded in confirmation. Amelia shook her head and said, "Oh, how my head hurts! The last thing I remember is that I was going back to you, and I suddenly saw this chair, and I felt exhausted. It was as if I heard a voice too. Gino, the voice sounded like yours. He said there is no problem and that I can sit and rest for a minute. Then..." Amelia paused for a moment as if she did not want to continue talking. She finally said, "I do not remember what happened next clearly. I was sitting, and I felt someone was hugging me; something held my hand tightly too."

"Call it superstition or whatever, but these chairs have a problem!" said Renzo, firmly, "There is a dangerous and deadly force in them! That's why Dr. Umanita said we shouldn't sit on them!"

"Look, I don't think anything strange happened here. Amelia hasn't eaten anything since last night, and she's tired. There is nothing mysterious about this." said Gino to calm them down.

Renzo said, "You think? Well, if so, let's try. This chair cannot be taken from here to the first floor, and let's move on from the

65

question of how it got here in the first place. It's time to do a test!"

Renzo said this and pulled out a knife from behind his back! Gino was shocked because Renzo did not look like someone who would carry a knife! Then he said,

"What are you doing? We still do not know what we are dealing with here!"

Renzo put the knife back in his belt and didn't injure or break the chair. Gino showed the most sensible behavior. He quickly grabbed Renzo and pushed him away from the chair. Gino said,

"I do not know if we are asleep or awake, but a strange thing is happening here! We have to go up as soon as possible!"

Renzo and Amelia moved behind him, and the three of them hurried toward the entrance. After crossing it, they proceeded to the hall, which now looked much darker with one flashlight. It was only in the middle of the hall that Renzo said,

"Gino, we went through a different corridor!"

Gino raised his lantern and saw that the tables were covered with various objects and bundles of paper. He quickly realized Renzo was right. All three turned back only to find that behind them was a row of doors. It was not clear from which they entered. The three of them looked at each other, and it was Amelia who finally said in a tired tone what everyone was afraid of,

"Guys, I think we're lost!"

Renzo growled when he saw a chair, "Again, one of these cursed chairs, I am getting upset when I see them!" Said Renzo.

"Don't worry, it's just a chair," said Gino, shocked by Renzo's angry reaction.

"Don't worry?! We will all die here if we do nothing!" said Renzo.

"Look, there's a door!" said Gino, "Maybe this is our way back!" They opened the door, and it led to another room that was a little bigger than the previous one and was filled with piles of scrolled paper in the middle of the room. Amelia picked one up and opened it. "Strange, it is written in Hieroglyphics!" said Amelia, "I mean, maybe these are old?"

"I do not think so," said Gino, "In this moisture, any kind of paper and papyrus would rot and disappear quickly."

"But there is no doubt that these are made of paper," said Amelia, "Feel its texture!"

Gino and Renzo took turns touched it, and shook their heads in surprise. There were two other doors in that room, each of which led to another room. Renzo turned on his flashlight and entered one of them. Gino and Amelia entered the second room and found themselves in a large hall with large tables. There was an extinguished torch. Gino lit it. They saw that this hall also had semi-open doors that connected to other rooms. On the tables was a complete set of chemical tools: glass tubes and a collection of laboratory objects that seemed to have been taken out of the Museum of the History of Medieval Science! On some tables were large glasses full of alcohol with dried creatures floating inside.

Gino approached one of them, and when he saw the hardened carcass of a feathered animal that looked like a reptile, he made a startling sound, "Wow..." Gino turned to show the glass to Amelia but saw that she was standing sadly and frustrated to say something.

"Amelia, is something wrong?" asked Gino.

Amelia said threateningly, "Honestly, Renzo caught us red-handed! Do you think that he will tell others about what we were talking about? If they find out, they will kill us at an opportune time to be safe!"

Gino was so eager to keep talking that he forgot had forgotten the strange things around him and suddenly realized the danger they were in because of that conversation. He asked,

"Well, what do you want to do?"

"I'll talk to Renzo and distract him, and at the right moment, you hit him in the head with something heavy! When we return, we will tell others that he was waiting for us upstairs and we did not see him on our way back!" said Amelia.

Amelia could no longer contain her excitement! She quickly snatched something like a copper pipe from the table and handed it to Gino, and said,

"All of this will be for us! All these treasures!"

Suddenly, a loud and terrible sound filled the space. It sounded like a massive explosion. A flash of light illuminated the room for half a second. The sound of the explosion was loud and confusing. Gino felt a strange pain in his chest as if someone kicked him in the chest! Pain with an intense sense of burning! The copper pipe fell from his hand, and an annoying sound filled the space. He put his hand on his chest. It was wet! Amelia came up to him and turned on the light. His whole chest was full of blood! He was shot and could not breathe. He was suffocating and was drowning in his blood. He fell to the ground and died a moment later. Amelia was completely confused and shocked! She did not know what just happened. She sat on the ground next to Gino's body and checked his pulse. Nothing! She looked around. A strange feeling of loneliness overwhelmed her. Suddenly, she saw Renzo coming out of a dark corner with a gun in his hand that was aimed at her! Amelia wanted to run, but Renzo said, "Don't move!" Then, he moved forward and kicked the copper pipe with his foot far away.

"Why did you shoot him?" asked Amelia angrily, "He meant you no harm!"

"Because I did not want to be your victim!" said Renzo.

Amelia realized that Renzo heard their conversation and that he might kill her too, so she quickly calmed down and said,

"Then why didn't you shoot me too?"

"It's a pity to kill a beautiful doll-like you!" said Renzo.

Renzo knew that if Amelia knew his intentions, accomplishing his plan would become much harder. Hence, he pretended that he meant her no harm and was attracted to her! He said to Amelia in a serious tone,

"Get up, go to the wall, and put your hands on the wall. If you do something else or if your hand gets off the wall for a moment, I guarantee I will shoot you!"

Amelia was pleased when she thought Renzo would not kill her and that she might have a chance to kill Renzo or escape from him, even if it meant she had to distract Renzo sexually. So, she eagerly raised her hands and placed them on the wall. Then, she said to Renzo,

"You know, Gino and I were not that close anyway!"

Renzo pointed his gun at Amelia and bent down to take Gino's shoelaces and use them to tie Amelia's hands. He said,

"I know after killing me, it was his turn. But Gino was stupid enough to think you would share this treasure with anyone! From the first moment that I saw you, I felt what a dangerous animal you are. When you two left and came downstairs, I sat down on the same dark wooden chair again, and the voice that resembled my lover's voice told me about your plan! When I heard your conversation, I knew that the voice told me the truth and that the only way to save me and get me out of here alive is to…" and he stopped talking.

"What is the only way?" asked Amelia.

"Put your hands on your back without provoking me to shoot you!" said Renzo, holding the shoelaces.

Amelia pulled her hands slightly off the wall and said that she could not get intimate with her hands tied. She also asked Renzo where he got the gun, but she didn't receive any response. Suddenly, Amelia remembered the sharp chemical glasses on the table that she could use to cut open the shoelaces and stab Renzo!

"I just need to get close enough to the table somehow!" thought Amelia to herself.

"Why? It's even better this way!" said Renzo.

Amelia knew she had no other choice. So, she let him tie her hands behind her back. Renzo tied her hands behind with one of the straps and then tied her feet with the other one. Amelia asked him again,

"What are you going to do with me?!"

"Dear! Having a relationship with you will not save my life! But killing you will for sure!" said Renzo.

He went to the alchemy table and threw everything on it on the floor. It was as if he read Amelia's mind! A harsh sound caused by objects falling on the ground filled the space and was echoed in the great hall. Amelia was now more desperate than ever! Her hands and feet were tied now, and no glassware was left on the table to use for defense.

"Then why didn't you shoot me like you did, Gino?" shouted Amelia. She was resisting and screaming as he pushed her to the table and threw her on it.

"Because that voice told me how to take out your heart while you are alive! This is the only way to unlock my destiny. Otherwise, others will kill me and put me on one of the chairs unless I act according to the directions of that voice!"

Renzo said this and pulled his knife out of the back of his pants, and raised it. Amelia cried and screamed and begged for help, jumping up and down like a fish out of water. She was shouting,

"Someone helps me! Please!" Her voice echoed loudly inside the hall.

Renzo stood there, knife in hand, and watched as Amelia screamed and begged. Renzo seemed to have no empathy for her cries and pleas. He punched her hard in the face, which left her dizzy and confused. She was lying on her back with her hands tied behind her back and stared at the ceiling. The events of the past few days paraded in front of her eyes. He suddenly thought about how she ended up at the lowest point of the building. At the same time, he could easily have one-sixth of the floors' treasures above the basement and stay alive! Why did she come to this cursed underground? For greed? For more property? And this is the sad end of her life story!

Renzo tore Amelia's shirt with his knife. Amelia accepted her fate and remained motionless and silently shed tears. Renzo split her chest open with his blade. the scene of that thick blood coming out of Amelia's chest and hearing her screams disoriented Renzo, and he said, "Oh, oh!" He trembled, and the flashlight he was holding in his mouth to see better fell to the ground and broke with a loud noise. The light went out!

Because of this, Renzo could not see Amelia's heart inside her chest anymore and could not find it. Amelia stared at his hands in disbelief and screamed in agonizing pain. Renzo dropped the blood-soaked knife on the table. He looked at Amelia's face under the last left lantern's light and said, "It's almost over!" He then dipped his hand into her torn chest to find her heart. Renzo then pulled her heart out of her chest while beating and cut the veins and placed it on her chest. And so he killed Amelia. Then, according to the voice's order, he placed Amelia and Gino's bodies on two dark chairs while they were soaked in blood. Then, he moved towards the entrance to go up the stairs.

"What a disturbing story!" Johnna said while her face showed she got frightened.

"Did she die?!" Sara asked.

"Yes, she died on that table!" said Ghiaccio while nodding.

"To be honest, I don't think any part of this story is real!" Damen said mockingly.

"You will see after I show you the proof of it at the end!" said Ghiaccio with a smile.

Everybody was shocked at first because of the story itself and then because of the directness of Ghiaccio!

"Do you guys have popcorn or something salty?" asked Dane.

"Yes, give me a second, but don't start till I come back!" said Sara, then she got up and went toward the kitchen and brought back a bunch of snacks.

"Would you like some Whiskey?" Richard asked Ghiaccio.

"Sure!" replied Ghiaccio.

Richard got up and filled up a glass for Ghiaccio, and then he filled others' glasses as well with the fine Whiskey he loved.

Richard drank a bit of his Whiskey and said, "This story is chilling! I really want to know how it ends!"

"Me too," said Randall. He exhaled deeply and continued looking at Damen, "Definitely not boring!"

71

Chapter 7

Karmelo paused in the second basement. Now that he was out of the lower floor's darkness, the candle lamps of this floor looked brighter than before. He remembered the valuables on this floor and was tempted to take another look at them. On the other hand, he wanted to get to the open-air sooner and get the nightmares of this adventurous day out of his mind. Ercole heard his footsteps and walked slowly to see who his next victim was!

Karmelo was thinking about leaving or staying when he heard the rushing footsteps of someone coming down the stairs. He walked up the stairs and accidentally hit Ercole, who was running down the stairs. Karmelo grabbed him and prevented him from falling. Then he said,

"Hey! what are you doing? Slower!"

"Run, run," said Ercole, out of breath, "He is coming! He has a knife! He killed Emma with it and is looking for the rest of us!"

Ercole didn't know whether Karmelo knew about Emma's murder or not, and he wanted to buy time to get Karmelo and the others out of the way at the right moment.

"Who is coming?!" asked Karmelo.

"The masked man! the masked man is after us!" said Ercole, "He has a knife!"

"Who is the masked man?! We did not have a masked man here!" asked Karmelo.

"I don't know who he is!" said Ercole, "I just saw him stab Emma and kill her and put her on one of those chairs upstairs where the paintings are! He grabbed Emma and stabbed her in the chest! I saw him myself! He killed the poor woman and put her on one of the chairs!"

Karmelo thought for a moment that Dr. Umanita hired a killer to kill them if they did not honor their promise. He frowned and said,

"Can you tell me what you were doing when this happened?! I did not understand anything!"

Then, he looked inside the hallway. There was no sign of the masked man with his dreadful knife! For a moment, it seemed as if Ercole was talking nonsense! Ercole shouted,

"Am I speaking in a different language?! What did you not understand? I said the masked man is a murderer! He sat in front of one of the chairs for a while, blocked Emma and me, and didn't let us out of the basement! I saw Emma drowning in her blood! Then he threw her on one of the chairs!"

"Well, why did he put her on the chair?" asked Karmelo, who seemed to be afraid, "You mean he kills everyone who is in the basement?"

"Yeah, he's a killer!! said Ercole, "He killed Emma!"

"But why would anyone do that?!" Said Karmelo, who still did not believe everything. He continued, "Logically, he should be as afraid of these chairs as we are! Unless…"

Ercole shouted, "I don't know what that madman thinks! He was looking for me to kill me too! He thought that I was in the front room in which Emma was killed. When he came back and saw me, he followed me with his knife! Then, I came down the stairs!"

Karmelo thought to himself that Ercole must have seen something. Although he felt the heat of those chairs, too, it was still hard for him to believe what Ercole was saying. Karmelo thought that he should've been there by now if there was such a masked man. So, he asked,

"Then where is this masked man?!"

"He probably heard you and is hiding somewhere!" said Ercole.

Karmelo searched a bit in the basement and finally found what he was looking for. He showed Ercole a long, wide sword he found and said,

"Well, don't worry anymore! You see, I was a boxing champion! I knocked out a lot of boxers, so don't be afraid! A masked man cannot hurt you when I'm around!"

73

Ercole was a little scared but tried to smile when he saw the sword in Karmelo's hand. Karmelo was encouraged to see Ercole's smile, and after a bit of digging, he found a full armor and put it all on! But because they were so heavy and difficult to move in, he took them off piece by piece, leaving only a broad sword in his hand and a horned helmet on his head. However, he was anxious and refused to go up the stairs. He thought that the masked man might have made a trap for them up there, and as soon as they climb up the stairs, he would kill them. Finally, since Ercole also said that going up was a bad idea, Karmelo was convinced to stay on the same floor for a while, and if the masked man did not come down, the two would go up. Fifteen minutes later, Ercole found a long dagger and a beautiful silver shield. He looked like an old animated clown! He was mocking Karmelo in his head and was laughing at him in his head! He then told Karmelo to follow him up the stairs, and they both walked up the stairs. Ercole had no lights on. He did not think the rest of the heirs could be upstairs. So, without hesitation, he searched the first floor of the basement.

Karmelo, who was sitting in a dark corner of the basement for a while and his arms and legs were numb at that point, shook them as he saw Ercole walking in front of him and moved forward with his long, fierce sword. They got separated next to a giant marble statue of a dragon, according to Ercole's plan. Karmelo went in one direction and Ercole the other. Karmelo saw Ercole sheltering in the shadow of a large shelf full of various tools and anxiously watching his surroundings. Karmelo went to Emma's room, and as he turned his sword over his head, he shouted,

"I know you are there! Come out before I tear you to pieces!"

Ercole was behind Karmelo now and hid in a corner. Karmelo saw his shadow and looked in his direction. When he realized that Karmelo saw him, he got out of his hiding corner. Ercole, with the shield in his hand, looked like a dangerous creature! Karmelo looked anxious because, in their calculations, Ercole shouldn't be there. Karmelo said,

"What are you doing here?! I thought you were the masked man!"

"I go from this side, you go from the other side, and whenever you see him, shout and I will come and help you!" Said Ercole.

When Karmelo turned his back to Ercole, Ercole raised his dagger and said under his breath,

"Young misguided miserable man! You do not understand what is happening! The dark chairs chose me! They chose me to inherit Dr. Umanita's wealth! That is why you all have to die! I am the masked man, you fool!"

Ercole said this and rushed towards Karmelo from behind. He tried to decapitate him from behind, but his dagger first hit the horn on Karmelo's helmet and then scratched the back of his neck. Karmelo turned back to see what just happened. At first, he thought Ercole was jokingly scaring him, so he stood up and shouted,

"Have you lost your mind?! You crazy old man!"

But Ercole continued to shout and run toward him, and there was no sign of a masked man! So Karmelo got scared and tried to escape. But Ercole reached him from behind and raised his dagger to stab him in the back. As Ercole ran and approached Karmelo, his foot got stuck to the edge of the carpet, and he lost his balance. His dagger hit Karmelo in the back and cut it open, and Ercole fell on the ground on his face. Karmelo screamed and fell to the ground. Blood gushed from his back. He was screaming in pain and pleading. He turned in that pain and saw Ercole standing over his head with his dagger on his neck.

"Get up!" said Ercole like a bully, "But if you make a wrong move, I will cut your throat!"

Despite the unbearable misery and pain, Karmelo tried to stand up but froze in pain while he was half-sited. Ercole's shield remained on the ground. Without removing his dagger from Karmelo's neck, Ercole moved and stood in front of him. Karmelo suddenly cried,

"No! No! Ercole! What are you doing?! I was wrong to come here in the first place! If you let me go, I promise not ever to come back!"

Despite the pain, Karmelo continued to beg in despair. Ercole stared at him with no empathy and said, "No! Do not pretend to be innocent!" Ercole hit Karmelo in the chest and knocked him to the ground. Karmelo said with great difficulty,

"You ignorant coward!" and died right away.

Ercole smiled happily and said, "It can't get any better!" He thought to himself, "We were going room to room for the past hour!"

He had hurried from room to room to hunt Karmelo at the right time, and that made him tired. Ercole then lifted Karmelo's body and dragged it into the hall to place it on one of the chairs. He thought to himself that he must have proved his loyalty to the chairs by now. He suddenly remembered three other people that he had to kill to live happily ever after! So, he went to the second basement and hid next to a large statue and waited for the rest of the group!

Renzo was trying to find his way back to the upper floor with great difficulty. He was parched and was going room after room to find his way. The rooms did not have any comprehensible floor plan. Even their shape was not regular. There were pentagonal, hexagonal, or even shapeless rooms that open with doors to adjoining rooms. There was a set of things in each room, which had nothing to do with the previous and the next room.

In one room, a complete set of replicas of old ships was mounted on wooden platforms. In another, a pile of kitchen utensils could be found. There was another room, the floor of which was covered with thick yellow velvet, and dozens of crystal balls were placed on it. In all this nonsense, dark chairs were visible from time to time. There was no indication of the extent of these rooms. He thought he was moving in a certain direction, but the rooms did not seem to end anywhere. But he did not pass through any room twice. The only light he had was a lantern left from Amelia. The oil from Gino's lantern ran out some time ago. He lost his flashlight too when he was killing Amelia. This lantern's dim light seemed to be enough to show the horrible scenery in one of the rooms. Renzo opened the door and entered without any hesitation, as usual. But suddenly, he froze with utter fear! He saw under the light of the lantern the shadow of a child! But when he looked closer, he saw a skeleton with remains of strange clothes on it. The skeleton had long white hair and a colorful necklace around its neckbones, indicating that it was once a small older woman. Renzo stared in amazement and fear! The older woman was tied to a pillar. There was a large marble pillar behind the skeleton. There was a large petal at the end of the pillar, and a goat statue appeared on it. Thick chains were wrapped around the skeleton that tied it to the pillar. A delicate, old-fashioned golden lock on the chain caught Renzo's eye.

    Renzo bent down and picked something up. Then he looked at it carefully under the light of the lantern. It was a golden key out of the skeleton's reach and placed on the doorstep. Renzo said to himself,

"Who could have done this?! This poor old woman was chained to this pillar and left to die out of hunger and thirst!" Then he suddenly remembered that this could be Dr. Umanita's great-grandmother.

"I don't think this was a murder!" he said to himself, "I heard that Dr. Umanita's great-grandmother committed suicide in the basement of their house, and her body was never found. When I heard this story, I never thought they meant a basement so deep into the ground! She probably chained herself to this pillar, and through the key over here, so she couldn't reach it! But that doesn't mean this skeleton necessarily belongs to her. Maybe she committed suicide in the upper basement. I heard that she was one of the few people who dared to go to the basement, in which, generation after generation, no one dared to set foot!

She probably saw something fearsome and had to commit suicide here. But there are a thousand ways to commit suicide. It is extraordinary for a person to starve herself to death like this! Maybe she didn't want to commit suicide? She just hoped someone would come and unlock the chains. Maybe she was afraid of getting lost in this basement? But she could keep walking until she was exhausted from hunger and thirst and not torment herself like this! But why? What is so terrible about sitting in those chairs that the older woman preferred to die like this? Of course, I saw what happened! Those chairs tempt people to sit down! They were forcing Amelia and Gino to kill me! Sooner or later, someone like this older woman who is lost here alone will give up and sit on one of those chairs. Yes, she locked herself here out of fear of doing just that! True, the chairs or the voice may have asked her to kill a member of her family, so she chained herself down here. What then?"

    Suddenly, Renzo remembered that he felt exhausted when he was sitting in a chair. He felt like he was falling into a very heavy sleep.

77

Of course, there was another strange feeling, too, as if he had entered a large family. As if he was uniting with his family after a long time. He thought that family could be the ones who sat in the chairs long ago. Maybe that's what tempts people to sit in the chairs. Then he thought to himself,

"Did those chairs steal people's souls from them? But why? I do not understand. Why should a chair want people to sit in it, and why do people who sit in it are transformed in a way? Maybe these are more than just enchanted chairs that I do not know about?"

Suddenly, fear-filled Renzo's whole being, and he began to tremble. Then he said to himself,

"No, they are just chairs made by a sorcerer or something! Only this! They seem to bite anyone who sits on them so that he could no longer destroy the chairs. I think they are good chairs! They are the best chairs I have ever seen! I think of them as dangerous creatures while they saved my life! Who knew how Gino and Amelia wanted to kill me! And all that just to get wealthy!"

Then he said in a philosophical tone that if anyone was there, they could hear too, "Yes! These chairs are good creatures! Chairs that are so comfortable! Well, their work is known! We have to sit on them, without moving, without getting up and doing anything! That is why they are so comfortable! A chair is made for this! Did I find a crystallized philosophical concept in Dr. Umanita's basement? I think I'm losing it!" he thought, frightened, "These are just chairs, wooden and German, and of course heavy and real. Something must have happened that they turned into magical and strange things!"

Ercole waited impatiently for the others to come from their basement exploration. He was in a large space, squatting on the ground next to a big statue. All of the treasures in those mysterious basements paraded before his eyes! But there was a barrier between him and the golden and eye-catching masses of treasures. Something terrible and scary that could destroy him and take away all his happiness: Others! They wanted his treasure! Suddenly, his eyes got heavy, and he fell into a deep sleep.

He dreamed that a row of dark chairs, like a line of bloodthirsty soldiers, stood between him and the things he loved! At first glance, the dark chairs looked the same way they always did: Stylish, wooden, clean, and comfortable! But as he got closer, something seemed unusual about them, but he could not figure out what it was. He knew he had to sit on chairs to reach the treasures. Suddenly, a voice caught his attention. It sounded like the wind. It was as if the wind is howling through the foliage of the garden trees. He felt his hair stood up on the back of his neck! He saw someone standing in front of him! It was Dr. Umanita standing behind the chairs, looking at him with a smile! He was much younger than the last time Ercole saw him. It was almost like the time when Ercole had trouble framing him. There was no fear in Dr. Umanita's eyes, just like then. There was only a kind sympathy in his eyes now!

"Ercole, do you remember how you came into our family?!" asked Dr. Umanita.

Ercole closed his eyes so he wouldn't see and hear anything else. But he heard his voice again. Magically, even though he closed his eyes, he could see Dr. Umanita in front of him and hear his words as clear as before! Dr. Umanita said,

"Did you forget your dad? Did you forget how much I helped you and your family? Don't you remember I was the one who got your birth certificate for you and put my name on you? Don't you remember you didn't have a name before?"

Ercole was sweating and was scared. He tried to forget all this. In his nightmares, his painful memories always began after this sentence. The memory of when they were homeless. He had just come to the city from the village with his illiterate father, helpless mother, and four little brothers and sisters. They had to sleep on the street at night and struggle with dogs and beggars to find a place to sleep. However, it wasn't a nightmare this time! He opened his eyes and saw the doctor standing in front of him and looking at him with the same smile! The doctor said,

"My dear son! get out of this house before another tragedy happens! Leave this house and do not look behind you! Like others, you failed the test in this house! Get out of here before your time runs out!"

"No! No! I waited every minute of my life for this moment! I'm not leaving here now! This is all mine! I will sit on the chairs again if I have to! Those chairs have no defects! They are strong and kind! I love them! They support me!" shouted Ercole.

Dr. Umanita slowly disappeared, but before that, he pointed to the chairs. Ercole looked at chairs and watched in horror as the chairs changed shape. There was a fire like molten iron on their surface! Eyes of different people who sat on these chairs at different times, with different thoughts and desires, appeared on the chairs' liquefied and heated surface! It was as if different parts of human bodies were coming out of the chairs' corners! From the middle of a chair, a sketch of a male face appeared, as if it was trapped behind that molten surface and was trying to get out of it by pressing its face against it!

Similarly, a seductive female head was formed on a different chair that was trying to get out! Worst of all were the mouths! Lips and mouths that appeared like delicate incisions on the dark wood of the chairs and were screaming! Some of them said things in foreign languages. Languages that Ercole did not understand. In the blink of an eye, the dark legions of waves turned into pulsating, disintegrating masses of torn, scattered bodies that pressed against each other, pressing against the transparent surface of the seats and trying to get out of it! Little by little, the sounds intensified. The sounds of crying and moaning, the sounds of crying that he had heard many times before in prison and always laughed at. But now, laughter could not reach his lips. It was then that he recognized a scream from the commotion. He knew this sound. It was Emma's voice! Ercole awoke in panic as his panting voice filled the air. He sharpened his ears to see if there was any noise around. Little by little, his memories flooded his mind. He got up with difficulty and quickly turned around.

Chapter 8

When Ercole went a little further, he saw a shelf full of different shoes. It was there that he heard the same voice that had spoken to him before, telling him that Renzo was approaching. He has a gun and a big knife. You have to cut off Renzo's tongue before killing him. Otherwise, you will not get out of here, and you will not own that infinite wealth! He asked the voice, "What about Amelia and Gino?" That voice replied, "Only Renzo is alive!" Ercole asked again, "Where is he now?" But did not hear an answer.

He was very excited that his job had become easier and closer to be completed! On the other hand, he thought Renzo must be so dangerous that he killed both Gino and Amelia. He turned to find a stick to strike Renzo's head. He headed downstairs slowly. He was happy to see Renzo's light from a distance. He had to hide in a good place to surprise Renzo! He hid at the top of the stairs next to a huge vase. There was no doubt that those strong and large chairs supported him and arranged events to achieve what he wanted! He had to stop Renzo from escaping. He squeezed the stick in his fist and pointed it towards the stairs. The handle of his stick got wet in his hands. His hands trembled, and it was as if his heart could stop with each sound of Renzo's footsteps! Sweat was pouring down his forehead. He wiped the sweat from his face. He thought to himself that he should not make the same mistake he did with Karmelo. He had to do the job much more accurately this time. As soon as Renzo's head appears, he should aim at the back of his neck. Because otherwise, Renzo is armed and will kill him like Amelia and Gino.

Renzo did not seem to be moving very fast, but the sound of his footsteps got closer and louder. Suddenly, Ercole noticed the top of Renzo's head. He paused to see Renzo's torso. Ercole quickly came out of hiding and attacked Renzo from the side. He hit Renzo on the back of the head in the blink of an eye and knocked him to the ground.

Renzo turned and looked at him with eyes strangely mixed with astonishment. A sigh came out of his mouth. He looked like he was dying. Ercole moved with agility. He knew he had to take Renzo to one of the chairs before he died and cut off his tongue. Ercole dropped his stick and cautiously dragged Renzo's bloody body through the bronze statues and shelves full of shoes and bags to the dark chair. Renzo, who lost a lot of blood, was lethargic and half-conscious. He was trying to resist falling asleep. Ercole thought to himself that he struck Renzo so hard that he could die at any moment, so he had to act fast. As Ercole was dragging Renzo to reach the chairs, he hit a side table and overturned a large bronze cup with a loud bang. Ercole picked Renzo up again and took him to the chairs. Ercole threw Renzo's half-dead body on the chair and immediately heard Renzo screaming in pain. He was waking up! Ercole turned as fast as he could and ran to his dagger to pick it up. Renzo realized what was happening to him and got up and ran away. Renzo ran aimlessly as he screamed. On his way, he overturned the shelves and cupboards to block Ercole, and Ercole followed him stubbornly.

Seeing Renzo's bloody body gave Ercole hope that he couldn't go far. As he ran, Renzo felt dizzy and struggled to aim at Ercole to shoot him. A dark chair in the corner-blocked his way. But Renzo paused and changed direction and went down the stairs. Darkness was a place where he felt much more comfortable than others. So, he had to go down as much as he could. When Ercole reached the dark stairs leading to the third basement, Renzo's footsteps could be heard. Ercole's clothes were soaked in sweat, and he was terrified of the basement's darkness, so he paused for a moment and then burst out laughing like a madman! His burst of laughter echoed on the lower floors. Renzo sat on the floor in a corner and said under his breath, "I can't anymore!" He leaned on the wall and said, "I can't, I can't take another step!" It was a while that the image of the dark chair had taken over his mind. He gently touched the back of his head with his hand. He felt a sharp pain. Then he looked at his blood-soaked hand. He saw that Ercole was standing at a distance, waiting to see a trace of Renzo's whereabouts, so he became completely motionless and hid there. The wound on his head was painful, and he felt he might faint at any moment! He did not know why Ercole attacked him and intended to kill him. He acted according to that voice. Those dark chairs no longer looked like something lovable and kind! Soon, he fell asleep!

After Renzo woke up, he remembered that when he was going up the stairs to find the rest of the heirs, he thought that maybe, if he sat on a chair, his thirst and hunger would disappear! He grinned and thought deeply about his stupidity! Then, he remembered his own house. It was much smaller than Dr. Umanita's house, but at least it was warm and bright, and no one wanted to kill him there! He stayed in that corner for a while, then grabbed the side of a shelf with his hand to stand up. Then, he said to himself,

> "It's close! I am sure that I will finally find a way to kill Ercole, even if it is at the cost of my own life!"

Renzo stumbled. He did not have the strength to walk, and he was confused. Ercole called him from the bottom of the third basement and said,

> "Come out, Renzo! I don't mean you any harm! I confused you with someone else! A masked man killed Emma and Karmelo and tried to kill me, but I ran away! When I saw you, I thought you were the masked man! Come out, and I don't want to hurt you! Let's leave here together!" He repeated his words louder one more time.

> "These lies are useless!" said Renzo to himself, desperately.

As Renzo sat down, he hit a porcelain vase by mistake, and it fell to the ground and broke. The sound of the broken vase filled the hall. Ercole realized where Renzo was hiding and tried to calm him down,

> "I know you are there!" said Ercole, "Believe me, I confused you with someone else, and I did not intend to harm you. I apologize for hurting you! We have to help each other to get out of this dungeon together, or we will be stuck here forever! Or the masked man will kill us! Now, I'm coming to you to talk and tell me if the masked man killed Amelia and Gino?"

Ercole slowly approached Renzo and was very careful not to provoke him so Renzo wouldn't shoot him! Renzo was ready to shoot with his hand on the trigger, and he did not believe a word of what Ercole just said.

> "Come close slowly and sit next to this statue. Stretch out your legs on the floor and put your hands on them so I can see them. If you move or your hands separate from your legs, I will shoot you immediately!"

> "Yes, of course, you have every right to be distrustful!" said Ercole.

He sat down next to the statue as Renzo ordered him. Renzo looked at him and said, "Well, tell me, what happened up there?"

Renzo was worn out in the past several hours. Time had passed in such a way that now he did not know how much time he had spent in the rooms of the basements. How many hours or days did he stay down there? He did not know! He spent hours finding a way back. He went from room to room with admirable determination! He had kicked aside the valuables in the rooms while stumbling. From room to room, from darkness to darkness, and from the middle of one set of objects to the middle of another set. No two rooms were alike. He saw nothing familiar except for those cursed dark chairs, which seemed to be everywhere. Renzo thought to himself why he couldn't find his way out was the impact of these chairs. But all of a sudden, he accidentally found the staircase! And then Ercole happened!

"We were sitting on the first floor in the basement waiting for you guys to come back," said Ercole, "And suddenly Emma screamed! Karmelo and I rushed to Emma's room and saw a masked man attacking her, stabbing her, and fleeing! Karmelo and I were scared and wanted to find him together. He attacked us and killed Karmelo with his dagger, and I fell on the ground, facedown. From then until you came upstairs, I waited by the stairs for him to come so I can surprise him, but I hit you instead of him by mistake! Please forgive me! I was sitting on one of the chairs when I heard a voice say to me, 'Get up! You should not sit on these chairs! Only the owner of all this property can sit on them!' I immediately got up and asked who he was! That voice told me that the only real owner of all of Dr. Umanita's assets was Renzo and that the curse would not end until he sat on a chair as a leader and everyone bowed to him; otherwise, no one will see the daylight ever again! Since then, I have been waiting for you to release us! All this wealth belongs only to you! Dr. Umanita knew this and wanted to destroy you on purpose!"

"Where is Emma now?" asked Renzo.

"She died of bleeding!" said Ercole and pretended to be upset! "Now, I will help you sit on one of these chairs, and then you have to be taken to the hospital for a CT scan of your head!"

"Okay, help me get up!" said Renzo, who now believed Ercole's deceptive words.

Ercole got up quietly, grabbed Renzo by the shoulder, and slowly lifted him off the floor, and they walked over to one of the chairs near them. He helped Renzo sit on it. Renzo was very dizzy and dropped his gun on the way to the chair, but he was no longer worried. When he sat down on the chair, Ercole went to his side and punched Renzo in the head with a sudden blow, knocking him unconscious. Then Ercole went and safely looked for the rope. He found a rope and tied Renzo's hands tightly behind his back. Ercole slapped him lightly on the face and said,

"Now tell me, why did you kill Gino and Amelia?"

Renzo stared at him confusedly and said under his breath, "Damn you cunning beast!"

Renzo pretended that he fainted to deceive Ercole, and Ercole believed it! He checked to see if Renzo was breathing and saw that he was still alive. Then Ercole said,

"He probably won't be alive for another ten minutes! I have to hurry! Then he went after the knife!"

Confused, Renzo suddenly thought of using the knife in his belt to cut the ropes and kill Ercole. He took out his knife and began cutting the ropes, and when Ercole came back with his knife, Renzo continued his work slowly.

Ercole grabbed Renzo by the jaw and pressed hard to open his mouth, then inserted the knife into Renzo's mouth so he wouldn't bite his hand. With his other hand, he grabbed Renzo's tongue tightly and pulled it out. He was careful not to upset the chair! Then, he moved the knife on Renzo's tongue. He felt nauseous from the vibrations of Renzo's tongue that he felt under the knife's blade. It was as if his tongue was an animal that wanted to escape death! As soon as the blade of the knife tore Renzo's tongue and inflicted a small wound on it, Renzo screamed as loud as he could! He cut the rope with difficulty, and the opening of his hand coincided with the complete amputation of his tongue. Blood gushed from his mouth. He was on the verge of insanity from the intensity of the pain and was screaming terribly. Suddenly, he plunged his knife into Ercole's chest, and both fell to the ground together.

Now the two of them were lying on the ground next to each other, twisting in pain. Renzo had to find a way out, and there seemed to be none! Ercole heard his heavy breathing in the humid and cold environment of the basement. He was starving and tired from the bleeding. His tongue was like a piece of wood from thirst, and he thought that he was approaching death quickly! He no longer felt happy! Because now he was losing everything, even his most precious wealth, his life! He was willing to go back to when he was in the lawyer's office and refuse this inheritance but stay alive! He could hear the squeaking laughter of the chair making fun of him. He then thought that if he could not get out of there alive, Renzo should not survive either. He moved his body, reached Renzo's gun with all his might, picked it up, and aimed it at him.

He felt foolish. He thought about how easy he'd lost everything. He pulled the trigger and shot Renzo in the head. Then, he laid on the ground and thought about his life events—day by day. He reviewed every moment of it. He was exhausted from the intensity of the bleeding. He had a sense of hatred that wanted everything to end sooner. He put the gun on his head with great difficulty, pulled the trigger, and ended his life.

"So, who was the woman you said went crazy?" asked Randall.

"It was Carina! She was innocent, so she never went to the basement! Only the greedy sinners and criminals went there! The basements and chairs were only for those who followed the lusts of the world and ruthlessly used every opportunity to deceive and tear others to pieces. That basement only attracted people who deserved to be destroyed! And all the victims were in that category!" Replied Ghiaccio.

"As a lawyer speaking, how can you say that?!" Said Damen, "You only know the end of their story, not who they were and what they did in life!"

Ghiaccio paused and replied, "Young man, a story is not just a story. It has a wider dimension. However, because they had always crossed every red line in their lives and considered themselves exceptional, they voluntarily entered that dark and endless basement on their own, thinking they will get out of there too! They were predators, wolves, hunters, hiding in sheep's clothing, and living in the community with others. Of course, all the basement did was releasing the wild wolf inside them. And they were the ones who did the rest and tore each other apart!"

Ghiaccio paused and took a deep breath. He said, "It was as if those chairs were chairs of justice and revenge!"

"Which part of those horrific events had anything to do with justice?!" said Damen, whose sense of advocacy was aroused! He continued, "We cannot clean someone's blood with another person's blood!"

Then, he looked at the others as if he was waiting for their approval and continued,

"Both are murder, and whether you were guilty or innocent in your lifetime. Blood, you do not clean with blood! Only water can clean blood!"

"No, that is not true! As a lawyer, you should know that water can never clean the blood on its own! When blood is shed, its effect always remains. Even if you erase its redness with water, its trace will remain. And, as for the justice you said, it is true that they have said that 'An eye for an makes the world blind,' but it is for crimes such as slapping someone, slander, or obscenity and the like, not murder! Please think of this example: If I do not cut the dry branches ruthlessly as a gardener, the whole plant will eventually dry out. It may then dry out the surrounding plants too. As human beings with thousands of years of life experiences, we know that people can escape the law by finding loopholes. What, then, is the task of justice? According to my father, having mercy on a leopard with sharp teeth is victimizing a defenseless sheep!" Replied Ghiaccio.

Everyone in the crowd was thinking deeply. Maybe they were checking their background to see if they deserved to go to that basement?! Or if they deserved to sit on those hot dark wooden chairs?!

Ghiaccio continued, "Of course, Dr. Umanita's heirs were punished in the same way that they secretly committed their crimes and sins in their daily life! This is the most trivial definition we have of justice! Of course, the concept of justice is much broader than human beings have understood!"

Sara, not believing this at all, asked, "I do not understand what kind of justice there is in Ercole's suicide!"

Ghiaccio replied with a smile, "Ercole's suicide was the end of the self-destruction pattern he lived in throughout his life. And got closer to his fate every second of his life. But he was unaware of it. He never thought he would kill himself one day until that last moment. If he listened to Dr. Umanita's warnings, it would not have ended as it did. Maybe, he even would be able to escape after Emma's murder. But his greed trapped him!"

"Then if that female survivor wasn't there, why did she lose her mind?!" asked Dane.

"Unfortunately, it was too much stress for Carina when she learned about how and why others committed those crimes and dirty deeds in those basements. She was so innocent that she was a stranger to the criminal world around her. So, she could not digest the criminal behavior of others! On the other hand, she might have needed a little professional help to find herself. Of course, she was released from the hospital after a short time and lived her life stronger than before. Maybe she also paid for a mistake!" replied Ghiaccio.

Johnna asked in surprise, "What mistake? You said that she had no role in the crimes of others!"

"Maybe her mistake was that she didn't choose the people around her more carefully! In short, everything has consequences!" replied Ghiaccio.

"I would love to see that woman and talk to her!" said Johnna, "There are many things I can learn from her!"

Ghiaccio looked straight into Johnna's eyes and said kindly, "That woman is in your mirror, every day!"

No one, not even Johnna, knew what Ghiaccio meant! Everyone thought maybe he was trying to refer to rebuilding one's self.

Johnna said in surprise, 'My mirror? I do not understand what you mean!'

Ghiaccio said kindly, 'Think about it for a while and give it time. It will make sense in your mind!'

Everyone looked at each other in surprise and wondered if Ghiaccio said a sarcastic sentence to Johnna! Johnna was the only person who did not have any academic and work-related success and was a housewife. Others thought that she was very lazy and useless and had no other use besides her incredible beauty! They thought even Ghiaccio was aware of her dullness and uselessness! They sometimes sneered at her in discussions and boasted that they were successful but that she was just a housewife!

But contrary to this popular belief, not only Johnna had a stunning appearance, but even more importantly, she had a wonderful personality, of which others were unaware. There is a saying that states, 'Only a jeweler knows the true value and the magnitude of gold and precious gemstones!' It means if one wants to know the true value of something, one must have expertise in it. Johnna was like a flower in a garden filled with poisonous plants that could, sooner or later, take away all her beauty with their obscure ugliness and actions.

Johnna was not highly educated, but she had moral qualities rarely found in the best of people. She did not miss any opportunity to help orphans, single mothers, the elderly, and the needy. She eagerly wanted to be kind and generous to everyone and make others happy. She prayed to God when she was alone and thanked him for his many blessings. She asked God for peace, friendship, prosperity, love, and health for everyone in the world, regardless of their skin color, race, ethnicity, or language. As if they are all members of her own family. Although she did not study in a university, she purified her heart, mind, and morals. She reflected on herself and her purpose on this planet. But she could never receive an honorary diploma for her moral achievements. Because, in essence, no earthly honorary diploma could reflect those accomplishments. Johnna had turned her home into a beautiful temple. There was no need for a mosque, church, synagogue, or Buddhist temple for her. She understood the true meaning of humanity and morality.

And because she reached a beautiful state, she could create beauty wherever she was. Although she did not follow any particular religion, she respected them all. The only thing she accepted in her heart was that this world has a very kind and merciful God who created this world beautifully. And she loved this God very much. Like her best friend, she imagined him to be her companion and guardian.

"Where is the proof of this story being true? Seems it's over!" asked Damen.

"It's not over! Wait for it!" replied Ghiaccio.

"Excuse me for asking this, how did your son die?!" asked Sara in a trembling voice as fear overcame her.

"My beautiful and kind son!" replied Ghiaccio, "He shined like a gem in the garden of my life! He was the fruit of my life! He was brutally slaughtered at an early age by an infernal couple, and then his body was thrown in the trash. A homeless man found his remains."

Sara became even more anxious. It was hard to believe. Then Ghiaccio, upset about having to talk about his son, looked at his watch. It was four-thirty on a Friday evening. He turned to the crowd and said,

"Of course, that was not the whole story. The main part of this story, which connects all these stories, remains to be clarified for you! Of course, I will tell you the rest of the story at a better time. I have to show you the photos and the documents and some of the recorded conversations so that the whole story is clear to you. Now I have to pack up and go!"

He said this and hurried out to the balcony and closed the large sliding door behind him. Suddenly, everyone felt very tired and very confused. They leaned back in their chairs and fell asleep. Only Richard was standing to fill his whisky glass again. But his head felt heavy and exhausted. He dropped the whisky bottle and dropped to his knees, then fell to the ground on his face. He closed his eyes and then opened them. Right in front of his eyes, right under the chair that Ghiaccio was sitting on, he saw a tear gas canister with Riot Control CS written on it! There was a clear gas coming out of it that was quickly fading into the air. Then he fell into a deep sleep just like the others. Silence overcame the space.

It was a tear gas canister that Ghiaccio had modified to put those people to sleep. He replaced the 'orthochlorobenzalmalononitrile' (CS) agent with a general anesthetic inhalable agent to put his audience to sleep. Ghiaccio took his simple Nokia mobile phone out of his pocket and dialed the first number on it on the balcony. After a moment, a voice across the line answered, "Yes?" and Ghiaccio said, "It's the time!" And then hung up.

After a while, he opened the large balcony doors and stayed on the balcony until the indoor air was fully ventilated. About 10 minutes later, a black van that belonged to an unidentified construction company entered the yard and parked in the parking lot. Two tall, well-groomed men in black military uniforms got out of the van.

One was African American, and the other was White American. They were Special Forces commando soldiers who had previously served in the US military. And after completing their service, Ghiaccio selected and hired them from among many people after long trials. Then, he sent them to different places to receive special training to be fully prepared for this mission! He intended to use them as assistants and his personal bodyguards. They were perfectly coordinated. They did everything without saying a word. It was as if they'd practiced it hundreds of times before. They pulled a stretcher out of the van and entered the house. Ghiaccio went to greet them, and as soon as he saw them, he gestured to them to follow him and said, "This way!" They went to the room where everyone was unconscious. He pointed to Johnna and said in a serious and demanding tone, "Take everyone but this lady! Be careful not to even touch her!" Ghiaccio looked at her innocent face with a father-like expression and said,

"You are going to be okay!"

There were tears in his eyes. He gently placed a small envelope in Johnna's hand. On the back of the envelope was written in beautiful handwriting, 'A gift from a friend!' Ghiaccio then pulled a plastic bag with a zipper out of his side pocket. He then bent down, picked up the grenade he threw under the chair, put it in the plastic bag, and closed it. He then put it in his pocket. His two assistants were named unit one and unit two. Unit one was the African American soldier that Ghiaccio hired first, and unit two was the other one who got hired after that and was under the command of unit one. They called each other numbers one and two, but Ghiaccio always called them with the word unit at the beginning of their number. Ghiaccio behaved quite like a powerful warlord. The assistants took a bag out from under the stretcher. They injected Sodium Thiopental solution into all the people except Johnna to keep them under anesthesia. The syringes were named in that bag, and there was a syringe with each person's name on it. Sodium Thiopental is mainly used to induce general anesthesia and sometimes alone as an intravenous anesthetic in short-term surgeries with minimal painful stimulation. After injecting anesthetics, units one and two worked together to place people on the stretcher they had brought in. Normally, each person is placed on one stretcher. But they raised the stretcher's side handles to the highest level and placed Randall and Damen on the stretcher together. It was as if they were loading potato sacks on the back of a truck! Unit two had a mocking look on his face and said, "Oh man!" Unit one looked at him seriously and sharply to make him end his mockery and continue working like a professional! Then, they hurriedly took the stretcher to the van and threw them into the van.

They handcuffed everyone and shackled their legs. They had to hurry because they could wake up before reaching the destination. In that case, the plan that Ghiaccio had prepared for them would not begin as he planned. So, they rushed into the house again. This time, they put Richard and Jonathan on the stretcher, in the same manner, put them in the van, and hurriedly tied their arms and legs like the previous ones. They went back inside, and this time, it was Dane and Sara's turn. They threw them on the stretcher, took them into the van, and tied their hands and feet. They quickly got in the van and left. As they left, Ghiaccio picked up all of their cellphones, went to the kitchen, and put them in the microwave. Then, he went into the master bedroom, opened the closet door, and turned off the modem and Internet router. He walked there as if he knew exactly what was where in the house! Then, he pulled out a small handheld radar that detected the Microwave Signal generator's location out of his pocket. It was the size of a cell phone with a screen at the top and a small keypad with several keys at the bottom. He took out the battery of his old Nokia phone to not intercept with the radar. Then, he turned on the radar, and the device started beeping from time to time.

He turned around himself once and stopped after seeing a red dot at the top of the screen. That device acted as a compass, except that instead of directions, it showed the Microwave Signals transmitter's generating point. He looked at one of the electrical outlets in front of him and walked to it. The closer he got, the shorter the time between the beeping sounds became. He placed his device next to an electrical outlet 12 inches to the right. Suddenly, the beeping sound became a continuous noise. He realized that this was exactly the point he was looking for. Then, he moved a shoulder-width away from the wall and stood sideways. He hit that part of the wall hard with the heel of his shoe and broke it. He took out the broken pieces of the wall and pulled out a black cubic box that was flashing from the wall. There were three wires connected to it. He removed the wire sockets and put the device in his pocket. Then, he pulled those wires tightly and separated them too, and put them in his pocket. That cubic box was a very powerful encrypter and signal transmitter that they secretly placed inside the house. It was crucial to separate and remove it. They put it there a few months ago when Ghiaccio worked there. One day, Ghiaccio was working, and the house owners were absent. The other cleaners worked hard and were distracted. So, he secretly brought his assistants into the house and entered them into the attic from inside the Garage.

They professionally installed sixteen pairs of white cameras the size of the bottom of a pen and microphones the size of a matchstick from inside the attic throughout the house. The cameras' white plastic, which was the color of the walls and their very small size, made it impossible for anyone to recognize the camera lenses with the naked eye and without infrared light. They used the ceilings and walls, and with great precision, they drilled very small holes so that the cameras were installed with special glue. This way, if someone came very close to them, they could only see a dot. They chose places like the corners of the rooms to cover the entire room. They connected a highly advanced Network Video Recorder (NVR) to all digital electronic elements without any internal memory. The electrical signals' output was then connected to a transmitter via a LAN cable, which used an advanced mobile wireless data system. After connecting it, a coaxial antenna cable and an electrical power supply were connected to that transmitter. And they sent it down from the empty hole inside the wall of the master bedroom. They then installed a cellular microwave antenna on the ceiling by removing the rotating fan mounted on the ceiling for Attic air conditioning. They connected the coaxial antenna cable to which the transmitter was connected and put the fan back in its place. Thus, through that antenna, the transmitter was never placed in the blind spot. Through the telecommunication network, the signals received from the NVR were sent to their receiving device.

And there, the information was received and stored live and in real-time. After installing that highly advanced system, they tested it with a laptop. They left immediately without anyone noticing their presence. Of course, they had installed the same system in the homes of other attendees at the party. And they recorded their lives moment by moment. It is noteworthy that, while Ghiaccio was telling that story, his assistants went to other people's houses and removed the transmitters they installed there from inside the attic. The reason for breaking the wall and removing the transmitter was not to leave an expensive device there. If the police were dragged there, in the process of inspecting those houses, they would find out through those transmitters that the people of that house were being monitored 24/7 by unknown people. But with the removal of those transmitters and the rest of the installed equipment, this theory would never be formed.

Now, if the investigators or forensic experts entered the attic, only one theory would remain. They definitely would think that one of the people that lived in the house was suffering from paranoia and secretly watched others. Moreover, because the transmitters' job was to send signals to an unknown location after encoding, by knowing the IMEI number of the devices connected to the telecommunication tower, the police could identify the receiver's connected device along with the receiver and find its geographical range. And that was not what Ghiaccio wanted!

Ghiaccio returned to the kitchen after removing the transmitter. He opened the kitchen microwave door, picked up the phones, and closed the door. Then, he walked over to Johnna and turned on her phone, and put it next to her. He put other people's phones in his pockets and hurried out of the house before Johnna regained consciousness. He went to his car in the parking lot and got in. He then placed the transmitter and the wires and cables he had removed from the house, along with the plastic bag containing the used grenade, on the back seat. He took an aluminum foil bag from inside the glove compartment and put all the cell phones inside it. He emptied a water bottle into the bag and zipped it. He started the car, took a deep breath, and looked at the house. He smiled contentedly and drove out the gate. After about twenty yards, he stopped, lowered the driver's window, and threw the aluminum foil envelope out in some boxwood bushes. He left feeling good about the process!

Chapter 9

A little while later, things were about to happen inside a very dark basement. The basement was empty of everything except for seven dark wooden chairs and a large wooden oval table. Of course, that table was very special and important! On that wooden table was a picture of an inlaid scale of justice with a large inscription on it, 'Only in God we trust!'

Above that oval table was a row of lamps like billiard tables. The only place they lit up was the table and the chairs around it, not their surrounding area. That way, only the tables and chairs could be seen in that room. Complete darkness surrounded the chairs. It was as if that darkness continued indefinitely. The chairs were arranged so that there were six chairs on one side of the table and one chair was on the other side. From the chairs' arrangement, it seemed that a chair that was separately on one side of the table was the position of the one in power, or rather, the position of the one who was going to pass judgment on others. There were two doors on the right and left in that room. Those were the vital doors that determined the fate of individuals! A flashing red light from a small CCTV camera in the corner of the room would catch one's eye in the absolute darkness.

Suddenly, the door on the left opened, and a little light almost lit up the room. Later, Ghiaccio's assistants entered the large room with the stretcher on which two individuals were lying down. They were Dane and Sara, who were thrown on their chairs like pieces of wood. They were placed in a way that they were facing each other on both sides of the table. Sara was on the first seat on the left, and Dane was on the right seat. They opened the handcuffs from one of their hands, and after passing it through a ring on the table, they tied those handcuffs to their hands again. The assistants then rushed back into the van and placed Richard and Jonathan on the stretcher in the same way.

Like the last time, they took Richard and Jonathan into that basement and threw them on two other chairs. Jonathan was sitting next to Dane to his right, and Richard was next to Jonathan to his right. Then, they hastily untied one of their hands from the handcuffs, passed the handcuffs through the metal rings on the table, and reattached them to their hands. They rushed out again, and now it was Randall and Damen's turn to enter the dreadful basement. They completed the previous process. Damen was placed on a chair next to Sara, exactly to her left. And Randall was between Damen and Richard. With their hands tight, they could no longer move, just like prisoners in maximum security prisons. The assistants left and went upstairs, which was the first floor. It was Ghiaccio's house. It was a very luxurious and aristocratic house, just like a palace! Ghiaccio owned it. Ghiaccio designed the house for a specific purpose! There was a secret entrance door that led to a large hall. Ghiaccio went to that hall after returning from Richard's house. He named the hall the 'Squadron.' That special room was full of large monitors, computer systems, and servers running. The assistants came in and sat down at their desks.

One of their tasks was to work with those systems. Ghiaccio was sitting in his chair, watching the process through a very large monitor attached to the wall in the middle of the hall. Sara, Damen, Randall, Richard, Jonathan, and Dane were still unconscious in the basement. Ghiaccio waited very patiently for them to wake up. About half an hour later, Jonathan was the first to regain consciousness. He looked around in surprise! He pulled his hand and saw that it was handcuffed to the table. He yelled at Richard and said, "Hey! Get up! Hey!" Richard slowly raised his head and looked at Jonathan. Richard's eyes were blurred. After a few moments, he said in a state of lethargy,

"What happened?!"

"I do not know where we are!" said Jonathan in shock and fear, "Who brought us here?" Then Jonathan shouted, "Hey, can you hear me?! Where are we?! Why did you tie our hands?! Open our hands quickly! I am a policeman. Do you know what the penalty of kidnapping a police officer is?!"

At the sound of his shouts, the others shook their heads and started to come back to consciousness. At first, Randall was blurting delusional statements, but they were very scared to see their situation after a short time. They experienced nausea, a drop in body temperature, and a drop in blood pressure due to anesthetics. Damen lost control of his bladder. The sound of droplets falling and the smell wafted through the air.

Jonathan said, "Oh, man, this is for real!"

Then Randall began to vomit and said in despair, "We were anesthetized! These are all side effects of anesthetics!" He said angrily, "Damn! Who did this?! Where are we?!"

Randall was an anesthesiologist and knew very well what had happened. He just did not know why it happened or what was going to happen.

"I remember pouring whisky when I felt dizzy," said Richard, "I fell to the ground and saw a cylindrical object emitting a white vapor under my gardener's seat. Just like the things the police throw in the movies that start smoking!"

"I have never seen a smoke grenade that is anesthetizing!" said Jonathan, "Also, why didn't we see the smoke? Damn, we're dealing with professionals!"

"I think Ghiaccio anesthetized us!" said Damen, "But why?"

Others asked, "Why did he do this?" Everyone had a theory. Damen said, "Maybe this is a game, and this way, he wants to tell us the rest of his story?!"

Jonathan said, "You idiot, who takes others hostage for telling a story?! He even made a hand grenade for us to anesthetize us! No! No! This must be related to one of our rivals!"

"If that's the case, they're in big trouble!" said Damen, "I will defeat them legally!"

"Our presence here is related to the story he told us!" said Sara, "I felt at the end of his story that he was seeking revenge. That's why I asked him how his son died!"

Suddenly, Jonathan noticed the camera light and said, "He is looking at us and listening to us!"

Ghiaccio, who was in the Squadron and was watching the whole affair, smiled as if he was playing poker and said, "The herd of hyenas that fell into the trap finally woke up!" He got up suddenly from his chair, and his assistants looked at him. Ghiaccio nodded to them and said, "It's the time!" His assistants immediately jumped out of their chairs and headed for the door. They all left the room together and entered the basement from the ramp that went down. The units opened the doors to the left, and Ghiaccio entered first. The corridor outside was very bright.

When the door opened, a flash of light suddenly filled the room. All the prisoners looked back to where the door was and, while the light was bothering their eyes, they wanted to see who entered. Ghiaccio and his assistants arrived. The prisoners were even more frightened when they saw the faces of the two assistants. They were completely silent and were breathing heavily. When the door was closed, the whole room, except for the tables and chairs, became dark again. Ghiaccio went to the remaining chair that was his chair. At the same time, one of his assistants got there faster and pulled back his chair with respect so that Ghiaccio could sit. He sat down and said, "Thank you!" His assistants were behind him to his right and left in the dark. Richard was the first to dare to speak,

"What does this mean? Who are you?"

He said in a demanding tone as if they were still inside his house and Ghiaccio was still his gardener,

"I will sue you in court! The police will surely follow you because we are missing! You were just my gardener! That's it! Do you want money?! Tell me! What do you want from us?!"

"I am the deputy police chief of the city!" said Jonathan, who dared to speak after Richard. He continued, "I guarantee you that you will not get out of this easily!"

While standing in the dark, Unit One reached out and placed a handgun on the table in front of Ghiaccio, pointed at the audience. The prisoners were waiting for Ghiaccio's answer but were confronted with the gun on the table and were surprised and scared, so they stayed quiet! Ghiaccio mockingly told them,

"You did whatever you wanted throughout your lousy lives! Until you entered this basement! You have no choice here! And you only follow my instructions! Otherwise, you will leave the game quickly! Or rather, for that person, the game will be over for you!" He then talked to them in a very serious tone. He said, "Game over means that you will be gutted alive, and all your intestines, kidneys, liver, and heart will be taken out, one by one. Just like what happened to my son."

Everyone just found out that Ghiaccio's son was one of their victims! And Sara was right! But they did not know which one of the victims was his son and how he found them! They were all very scared.

Even though they had many questions, they were silent for fear of the gun on the table.

Ghiaccio continued, "You started a game with me that we did not have the opportunity to finish. I call that game 'The game of human life!' When you were free and were tearing the society apart, you followed your own rules—the law of the jungle! Whoever was stronger, whoever was smarter, he won! It was enough to leave no trace behind! But now that you are in my basement, you have to play by my rules! I am more powerful than you now, both on earth and in this underworld! I'm smarter than you! So, the secret of your survival is in respecting my rules! Otherwise, as I said, you will be done for! And it is better to know that your names are legally registered in the manifesto of a flight to Cuba. People have flown there instead of you. So be aware, no one, I repeat, no one will come to your rescue!"

Then, he paused and said, "Well, the first rule here is that if you talk in this room again without my permission, it will be game over! If you decide to speak, raise your hand, and I will let you speak. You can only talk when you get permission! Rest assured, I'm not kidding! If I have not killed you yet, it's because you have to participate in this game! I only give one of you a chance to live! This is not like when you constantly caught me off when I was telling a story! If you think that I'm joking with you, try me! As your punishment, you will give your life!" Ghiaccio wanted to break their pride!

They were people who were completely free until hours ago and did whatever they wanted. They humiliated Ghiaccio when they repeatedly caught him off as he was speaking. Now, they had to get permission to speak from that same person!

"The second rule is that if your goal is to get out of here, you must follow my instructions precisely! Otherwise, it will be game over!"

Dane raised her hand in fear and asked for permission to speak. Ghiaccio said, "Yes?" Dane asked, "Excuse me for asking this, but they killed your child. What is my fault that I am here?! Please at least let me go!"

Ghiaccio said with a bitter laugh, "We will talk about each of you and your crimes in time! But now, why do I punish someone who breaks the law the same as the most sinful of you?!" He paused and said, "There is a famous saying in the army, and I like it a lot! It says, 'If someone makes a mistake in a military unit, everyone will be punished in that unit the same way. And if someone succeeds alone, he is the only one who gets rewarded!' In this game, you are on a battlefield! Only one of you will win, and the reward is freedom and life!"

The audience could see that this was a serious matter! They were trembling with fear like a willow tree. Randall raised his hand to get permission to speak. Ghiaccio said in a very cold and serious tone,

"What?!"

"Where is Johnna?" Randall asked in a trembling voice, pausing between each word.

Ghiaccio grinned at him and said, "Only sinners enter this basement! She was an angel trapped in the clutches of a wild hyena, you! She is none of your concern anymore. As I said, she was like a flower among thorns and weeds. As a gardener, I had a duty to destroy diseased and rotten plants so that healthy plants would not be harmed!"

Dane raised her hand again to ask permission to speak. Ghiaccio looked at her and said,

"Say it!"

"Who are you?!" asked Dana in a frightened manner, "I think you are a good person; why did you bring me here? I did not do you any harm! Why are you treating me like this? What was my sin that you did not leave me alone like Johnna?!"

Ghiaccio smiled bitterly again and said, "Are you in such a hurry to be killed?!" Then, he said to them, "The reason you are here is that the story I told you ends here! You started a game with someone you did not even know! Now, only one of you will leave this game alive—the only one who can play this game according to its law!"

Sara, who even doubted the story of Ghiaccio in her house and immediately asked him about his son, raised her hand to speak. Ghiaccio let her speak. Sara asked,

"Who are you, and how did we start the game of human life with you?!"

Chapter 10

"Okay, looks like you are too eager to learn the rest of the story!" Said Ghiaccio, "As I mentioned before, the story that I told you today is quite real! Some parts of it happened already, and some parts of it will happen here! I told you that the neighborhood where house number 17, which is an unlucky number in Italy and was located in the street called La punta dell'Iceberg. You know that in Italian, it means the tip of the iceberg, just like you, who hid all your dirty deeds underneath your pretty exterior, like an iceberg that most of it is hidden underwater! After all, the number 17 is very unfortunate in the Italian culture and a sign of a curse. Then I said that the name of the architect of Dr. Umanita's house was Nascita, which in Italian means birth. I also said that the office of Dr. Umanita lawyer was on Giustizia Street, which means justice in Italian. Umanita in Italian means humanity, which you have no idea what it is! As Dr. Umanita, humanity is dead to you! The legacy of Dr. Umanita is the heritage of humanity that has reached you. And those precious old books and manuscripts are the sciences left to humanity as a result of the many years of life on this planet that you learned in schools, universities, and books. Jewels are the precious people you met and lived with during your life. And the precious golden vessels are the same financial wealth that God has given you, but you spent all of that in wrong ways and then gained wealth in the same wrong ways! And those beautiful paintings are the beautiful sceneries and beautiful landscapes, which you could use and enjoy to the fullest. The only condition that Dr. Umanita, meaning humanity left for you, was not to enter the basement. Going into the basement in this story meant breaking the rules and social norms you were forbidden. But you shamelessly crossed the red lines one after another, and now you have reached the lowest and darkest part of your life story!

The chairs that were in the story are the chairs that you are sitting on now! You are the example of those who have decided to quit being compassionate human beings and turned into savage beasts! And with a deceptive appearance, you hunt the defenseless deer of our world! Now it is your turn to taste your own medicine! He paused and stared at the inlaid image on the table. Then he continued, "My real name is not Ghiaccio! It is rather a title that I have chosen for myself. In Italian, it means ice. My real name is Dr. Paul Umanita. I am the father of Joshua Umanita, whom you brutally killed, in addition to his fiancé, Clara."

When Sara heard this, she knew this is the end of her! She knew she would never see the sunlight again! She remembered Joshua well! Frightened, she fainted on Damen that was seated next to her. Damen shoved her away with his shoulder, and her head fell on the table. After a few moments, she came back to consciousness and lifted and shook her head. Ghiaccio thought to himself,

"These are even crueler than I thought! Damen did not even tolerate Sara's head on his shoulder when she fainted!"

Ghiaccio looked at Sara and said, "When you were in power, you were braver!" Then he said, "four years ago, my son's fiancé, Clara, went to see Dr. Richard Grinstein, the gynecologist, for severe pain in her abdomen. Richard saw her as a good prey, so just like his other victims, he made a sinister plan for her.

Richard falsely told her that she might have ovarian cancer, even though he found out with an ultrasound that her problem was not important and was probably just a change in her hormonal levels. But Richard said they had to do an ovarian biopsy to see if it was cancer. Clara was unaware of the procedure's difficulty, and Richard knew about Clara's Trypanophobia. So, Richard was able to intimidate and convince Clara that it would be best to have the procedure performed under anesthesia so she wouldn't feel any pain. He gave her an appointment. At that date and time, Richard was fully prepared to hunt her down. It was at that time that Dr. Randall Hershberger, the anesthesiologist, stepped in. The two beasts, who are now sitting here handcuffed, raped Clara after she was unconscious. Little did they know that Clara was a little skeptical of Richard's insistence on anesthesia. She was an intelligent girl and decided to have a voice recorder to know what happened during the operation. She was taken to the room before you two to get prepped for the procedure, and as she was

103

waiting for you, she hid the voice recorder somewhere in the room. After the procedure, when she woke up, she picked it up. When she got home and listened to the recorded voices, she heard that Richard and Randall asked the nurse to leave them and that she was not needed. And then they raped her. Clara immediately contacted Joshua and informed him of the matter. They then went to another gynecologist to clarify the concern.

The doctor told them with a simple ultrasound that Clara had no problem. The pain was probably due to rapid hormonal changes resulting from severe stress, which will get better with one course of a pill. Hearing this, they went to your office. But you denied everything. And you told them there was no biopsy, that she had hallucinations, and that you just did a simple routine examination. The same thing was also registered in your clinic system. Then, when you found out that they had evidence from you, you told them that it was better to go to the police station if they were upset! They were unaware of everything and were surprised that you told them to go to the police station, but they went there anyway. However, before they arrived, you called Jonathan, and he was waiting for them!" Ghiaccio pointed his finger at Jonathan and said, "Then, you took that recorder as evidence and said that you were going to follow up the matter, but you never did! When they came to you the next day, you told them that they did not give you any evidence and that they were deluded! But you saved the sound in that recorder to a flash memory, which was hidden behind a mirror in your house. Of course, others were certainly unaware of that! Jonathan collected evidence about all your activities to use as a lever of pressure on you in the day of need and to put you under pressure! Of course, I must say that I did not know about the existence of such a flash memory at first until Dane found out! When she came to your house for your secret affair, she found out about your secret.

One time, as you were taking a shower, she decided to take a look around! And after seeing the contents of the flash drive, she decided to keep a copy for herself! We saw it on camera, and we made a copy of it too! That's how we got all the CCTV video files of your underground clinic! Photos with descriptions of each victim; the number of bribes you have received;

Damen's connections to criminal gangs; addresses of the persons to whom you sold the victims' organs; And the amounts you received! We will get to them all later!

Joshua and Clara went to a lawyer and decided to sue. But Damen, your lawyer, despite being fully aware of the truth, managed to use Richard's fame and fortune to convince the judge that Joshua and Clara falsely accused Richard of scamming him! The judge dismissed the case in the absence of witnesses and evidence. Clara, whose lawyer told her she had no chance of winning, committed suicide by cutting her wrists. She died of severe and painful bleeding. Joshua then came to you for revenge, but you had him severely beaten in a dark alley by your gang-friends. After spending some time in the hospital and at home, he decided to find Richard's home address to visit his wife, Sara, and discuss the matter with her and ask for help. Sara pretended that the issue was very important to her! And that she will talk to her husband about it that night!

Sara told him that he should go to his clinic the day after to talk about it more together! I had just returned from Italy that day. Joshua explained everything to me in detail that night. I told him we had to go to the clinic together. But he told me that Sara is a very good and kind woman! 'His wife is very upset about this, and she will help me!' Joshua said to me. But I insisted that he should not go alone. Even before going to bed, I insisted that we go together. But the next day, because my sleep pattern wasn't back to normal yet from my trip to Italy, he left home when I was asleep. He went to your clinic, and I never saw him alive again. His mutilated body was found the next day next to a trash can by a homeless man. To not leave a trace of any medical personnel's involvement, you broke open his chest without anesthesia and with non-medical instruments. You removed his limbs as if he had been tortured by someone like street gangs to settle accounts. Because he was beaten and hospitalized before, the police did not doubt that he was involved in a street gang fight. They did not pursue the matter. Of course, you had to leave his body in the city. Because they complained to you and his disappearance would draw unnecessary attention to you. I am sure that DNA experts will find the remains of twenty-seven other victims in your underground clinic below your country house. Victims who were abducted by you for sexual and psychological abuse. You raped them and handed them over to your group's butcher to make money by mutilating them and selling their organs. You did the same thing you did with Joshua with a 10-year-old boy who was a student of Dane.

When you, Dane, got angry with him, you asked the child to stay and talk to you when the class was over. When you were alone with him, you took his finger and twisted it in the opposite direction so that it broke. Then, as the child screamed, you covered his mouth. You began to squeeze the innocent child's throat as hard as you could. Then you let go of his throat. You told the child that if he said anything to anyone, you have their home address, you will go to their house and will kill him and his family. The child believed you because he experienced your cruelty first hand a moment ago.

When he got home, he did not tell anyone about it. According to his medical record, he suffered from a broken finger for more than forty hours before his mother accidentally noticed the swelling in his hand. When she asked his child, the child told her that he fell on the way home. He lied because he was afraid for their lives. What a burden for a little boy! The next day, he came to school with a plaster cast on his hand. You, in fear that he might have revealed the matter, discussed it with Damen, and then he was taken hostage on the way home and was delivered to Damen in the trunk of a car. Damen gave him to Randall as a gift! After taking the child to the country house and raping and abusing him for hours, plucking his skin and nails, and burning him with a cigarette, he handed him over to Sara to take out his organs to be sold.

Three months later, the same thing happened again. This time, it was a ten-year-old girl who Dane picked up as she was returning home, and no one saw her again. But there is a video in which Damen takes the child out of the car and into the underground clinic.

Interestingly, Jonathan used to make a synopsis of those dirty deeds when you described them to each other! There were recordings in that flash memory of all of you explaining all your crimes with details in your gatherings. It was fascinating for me that Jonathan recorded you without you even noticing and kept all of them as evidence against you!

Damen told the story to Jonathon that after Dane tricked the child into her car, she suddenly brought an excuse and said they have to stop at her house very briefly before dropping off the girl at her destination.

After stopping at the house, Dane lured the child into the house under the pretext of helping her get her stuff inside. She then began beating and torturing the child with a whip. After that, she gave the child to Damen. Damen and Richard, loyal customers of a brothel called 'Caesar' that traffics girls between the ages of ten and fifteen saw this as a great gift. They took that innocent child to the country house. After she was brutally raped, she was handed over to Sara." Ghiaccio turned to Jonathan and told him, "You were the deputy police chief, and you should have been the fulcrum of society. Instead, after taking prostitutes to the country house and taking full advantage of them, of course violently, you handed them over to Sara to slaughter them!"

Then he told Jonathan, "After four years of following you, I was able to understand why others did what they did, but I never understood why you did what you did!"

Jonathan wanted to speak, so he raised his hand to get permission to speak. Ghiaccio replied, "Say it!" Jonathan asked,

"Well, after all that, what do you want? Do you want us to confess our sins? Do you want to hand us over to the federal police? Do you want to kill us?"

"I asked you why?" said Ghiaccio.

"I do not know exactly," said Jonathan, "I remember growing up in a good family. I always lived by the law, and that is why I wanted to enter the police force. Being a policeman was a value for me. Until I got to know these people. I changed little by little. Slowly, we began to cross the red lines. Surely, if I knew at first how far we were going to go, fear would have taken over my whole existence! But once you get into it, you no longer have a conscience to stop you! I do not know!" He took a deep breath and said, "What can I say? We are who we are!"

Then Ghiaccio said angrily, "You are a disgrace for humanity! Of course, I'm sure you can never understand the depth of the tragedy of your actions! Because your hearts have darkened, and there is no light in them anymore. Dark as this underground. One day, I felt like I was the happiest person on earth! Having my wife, whom I loved, and my son, who was the only fruit of my life, and the great family inheritance I had, I was nothing short of a happy human being. But suddenly, a tornado turned my whole life upside down. That was your tornado. I have been looking for you since that day. I followed your life moment by moment. I made this place just for you! Who knows, maybe after you, I will go after dirty people like you! You were supposed to serve people on earth. But greed and lust brought you here! How could you have mercy on others when you don't even have mercy on yourselves?!"

Then he pointed to Dane and said, "This woman has a secret affair with these two men next to her!" He pointed to Jonathan and Richard. Then, he pointed to Sara, who was on the other side of the table, and said, "This woman also secretly has an affair with the man next to her!" He then pointed to Randall and said, "This fellow hyena rapes and tortures children. Poor hyenas! They have more honor than you! I do not know of any beast that is as wild and predatory as you are!"

Then, he raised his right palm from the side. One of his assistants gave him the remote control of the projector. He started showing disgusting photos and slides and videos of their crimes. Part of it was obtained by tracking them down. Part of it was taken from Jonathan's flash memory. Part of it was public announcements and missing person postings. For about an hour, many videos were selected and demonstrated to confirm all of Ghiaccio's claims.

Those videos included: a video of a secret relationship at Richard's house between Damen and Sara; At Jonathon's house between Dane and Jonathon; At the Damen's house between Richard and Dane; Videos from the country house and the underground clinic CCTV cameras; Videos that Randall kept as a trophy; Pictures of twenty-seven different victims, which were taken to the entrance of the clinic by all of the people present with the exception of Dane; Missing persons ads posted after the victims went missing; 28 text files of Jonathan's description of how they committed their crimes, part with his own presence, and part with a description he had heard of others; Clara's audio file that Jonathan claimed he never received; Video of them negotiating prices with organ recipients; Video of their monthly meetings without Johnna, where they reported on their work and made decisions; Video of Johnna sitting alone on the floor at home, holding out her hands to the sky and praying and saying, 'O God! Thank you for your many blessings and kindness! O God, I ask you to give many blessings to all the people of the world, regardless of their skin color, race, or language, especially for orphans, single mothers, the elderly, and the needy! O God, I wish all people to be kind and generous to each other, make each other happy, and not harm each other! O God, I ask you for forgiveness, peace, friendship, love, prosperity, and health for everyone ...'

Seeing this video, everyone looked at each other in surprise! In the end, the photo of Joshua and Clara was shown. After a while, Ghiaccio turned off the projector to return his focus to the room. Richard raised his hand to speak, but Ghiaccio did not allow him to speak. He said,

"No! You cannot say a word!" Then he started talking and said, "It is better to go back to the game and its rules. There are seven rooms in this basement. Only two of these seven rooms are connected to the entrance hall, which is the seventh room. Only the one who reaches the last room can get out of there. This room has two doors. The left door through which you entered and the right door through which you must exit. When you enter through the door on the right, you will go to the next room.

There, each of you is given a walkie-talkie except one of you. There are a total of 5 walkie-talkies with the owner's name. Everyone should pick up their own device. Otherwise, the person who makes a mistake with the devices will leave the game cycle, and it will be a game over for him or her! In that case, my assistants will take that person to a special room immediately. There, with no anesthesia, he or she undergoes surgery, and your organs will be taken out, and you will be left there to die—a very painful death. So, remember, the choice is yours! Through walkie-talkies, you will be provided instructions that you must follow exactly..." He paused a little and repeated, "Follow exactly; otherwise, you will either be killed by others, or you will be automatically taken out of the game. Here, we hold a heart rate monitor bracelet that transmits your heart rate to our monitor.

If you open your bracelet, it means game over! The rooms are equipped with cameras and speakers. You will be given tools that you must put back in their place before you exit each room. If you take a tool or weapon with you to the next level, the game will be over for you, even if you destroy everyone else. Even if you succeed in achieving the target of a level outside of the given instructions, the game will still be over because you did not act according to the rules and following your own will! If the victim of any stage escapes the punishment of that stage, it will be game over for everyone other than them. The winner will be the only one who will survive. And that person will not need to get to the last step because then we will take the rest of you to the operating room. So, the winner will be released.

When the door opens on your right, the game is over if anyone stays in this room. You all have to go through the right door. After passing through each front door, it is impossible to return to the previous room. At the end of each step, the front door of the next room opens. There is a chair in each room. The victim needs to be punished according to the instructions and sit on the chair. The door will not open for you until the victim is seated on the chair. So, you go step by step. There is a set time at each stage. If you do not succeed by the end of that time, the victim wins. Jonathan raised his hand to ask a question. After getting permission, he said,

"Excuse me, I do not intend to insult you, I will act according to your rules, but what guarantee is there for us that in the end, you will release the remaining person or that he will not be killed by someone else like the story you told us?!"

Ghiaccio said with a smile, "If he is injured or killed by someone else, it is not related to the game process but your ability! On the other hand, I am the man of my word! In fact, from the first time you saw me, I told you what was going to happen! But you did not notice! Besides, you do not see Johnna here, do you?! She bought her freedom with her behavior! Now it's your turn to try!"

Jonathan, who was more physically fit as a police officer, was thrilled and hopeful because he knew more techniques than the others. He thought to himself that he would surely be saved. He kept reviewing the rules in his mind to make sure he follows the instructions. Whatever they might be.

Ghiaccio said, "Now if you have any questions about the game, ask!" A deadly silence filled the room. Then Dane begged,

"Please have mercy on me! Yes, I accept that I'm not a good person, but this is a horrible ending! Please give me a second chance to make up for my mistakes!"

"So, what about me?!" Damen said to Dane, "You wicked prostitute!"

Jonathan turned to Dane and said, "I should have known you long ago! You caused all our information to be leaked! Otherwise, only Sara and Richard would be punished!"

"If you have a complaint about the cruelty of this game, I have to refer you to the saying that goes, 'You should not have danced with wolves if you were afraid of getting torn apart!' Ghiaccio told the crowd in response to their pleas.

His assistants then tied the Heart Rate Monitor bracelets tightly around their hands. Ghiaccio said emphatically,

"Remember that the last person's bracelet can be opened only in the seventh room, and only by us! This key that I will put on the table is just to open your hands. But before that, you have to sign and leave your fingerprint on three sheets of white paper!"

Damen, the lawyer, raised his hand to get permission to speak and then asked, "What are these papers for?!"

Ghiaccio replied with a smile, "You will understand! Do not rush! However, if you do not sign and fingerprint, it will be game over! His assistants then placed three sheets of white paper in front of each of them. They took turns with a pen and a stamp pad in front of them, and they signed and fingerprinted the three sheets. Ghiaccio then placed the key on the table and said to the crowd, "Your legs will remain tied during the game! After we leave this room, you can open your hands. If you hit each other in this room, it will be game over! By the way, those papers are the power of attorney that transfers all your property to Johnna!"

Then, he placed a key on the table and quietly left the room with his assistants. They went upstairs to the Squadron room.

Chapter 11

When Johnna woke up in the house, she saw in disbelief that no one was by her side! There was no sign of her husband! Her friends were not there either! She was completely unaware of everything!

She was severely nauseous and dizzy from the anesthesia and sat still for a while, and stared at the wall in front of her. Then, she began to breathe rapidly to relieve her nausea. Johnna could not guess what happened there. The envelope that Ghiaccio placed in her hand fell to the ground and caught her attention. Soon, she was fully awake, and her symptoms of confusion and nausea decreased. Johnna remembered for a moment the Hollywood movies in which all the people of the city turn into zombies! She was extremely afraid that she was there alone. It was as if she was the only living thing in the whole wide world! There was no sound around her, and she suddenly thought of turning on the TV to see if it was an apocalypse! After turning the TV on, Johnna saw that everything was as usual in the world! She changed the channels, and nothing was changed! She picked up her cell phone next to her and called her husband, Randall. She heard the automated mobile network operator say that his device was turned off. Then, she thought of calling her mother, so she picked up the phone and started talking to her mother. Johnna didn't know whether to tell her or not, but everything seemed normal on the other side, so she decided it was best not to concern her mother by saying something. Johnna suddenly thought that maybe she fell asleep, and the others left the house to have fun without waking her up. That thought calmed her down. When she wanted to get up from her chair to drink some water, the envelope caught her eye again. Another thing that caught her eye was a whisky bottle on the floor, and whisky spilled on the carpet where Richard was pouring whisky before the anesthesia.

Johnna immediately thought that this could not be normal and became nervous once again. She picked up her cell phone and called each of her friends who were at the party. But to her surprise, everyone's cell phone was off! She took a deep breath and thought of calling the police. But before that, I bent down and picked up the envelope from the floor. On the back of the envelope was written in beautiful handwriting 'A gift from a friend!' Johnna thought to herself that maybe her friends left the envelope for her before leaving. After opening the envelope, she saw a flash memory with a letter and a business card in it. She looked at the top

113

of the letter in surprise and saw the words 'Dedicated to dear Johnna, on behalf of your friend, Ghiaccio!' This was not usually the literature that her friends or spouse would use! This could not be one of their annoying jokes! The letter read,

'Dear Johnna,

The story I told you today was true, with only one difference! As I said during the story, my parents are originally Italian. And I was one of the heirs of Dr. Umanita! I was the only one who refused to break the promise I made and did not betray Dr. Umanita's wishes in his will. I did not go to the basement. At the end of the story, I inherited all that wealth because I chose the path of honesty! I love you like my daughter, so you can think of me as a compassionate father! I suggest you always choose the path of honesty in your life!

I must inform you that one of the very basic definitions of justice is that everything must be in its own place. With all due respect, your place is not next to the people you have chosen as your spouse or friends! You have to find your right place and interact with people who have a pure heart like yourself! Otherwise, you may fall victim to the evil deeds of those around you! Even when you are unaware of those deeds, they can cause you trouble. This time, the Almighty God took pity on your pure heart and somehow put me in your way to free you from these people and get them out of your life! But know that you may not get a second chance! So, my dear daughter, be careful in the future to surround yourself with worthy individuals! I will tell you briefly about those around you and their deeds and actions so that I do not disturb your beautiful soul too much! But I must say in advance that sometimes knowing the truth, especially about the beasts who lived around you, can be very upsetting and painful. You must know that I believe in the purity of your soul in my heart, and I do not blame you for any part of what you are about to learn.

As I told you in that story, I had a very handsome son, with a very bright future ahead of him and a heart full of love for life and others. His name was Joshua. He dated a very beautiful, kind, and loving girl for two years. Her name was Clara. They got engaged and decided to get married soon. One day, Clara went to Dr. Richard Grinstein for sudden pain in her abdomen. Richard set a trap for her and falsely told her that she had ovarian cancer and needed a biopsy. After tricking her into believing she had to undergo the procedure, your husband and Dr. Randall Hershberger anesthetized Clara and raped her.

After the incident was revealed to Clara by a voice recorder, she brought it with her that day, and after informing Joshua, they tried to pursue it through legal channels. In the process, they found out that Clara didn't have cancer, and her pain was due to hormonal changes because of college stress! It was there that the police officer, Jonathan Hodge, stepped in and took the available evidence from them to "pursue" it. Instead, he hid the evidence and then denied its existence! Joshua and Clara were then forced to sue without evidence. It was there that Richard and Randall's lawyer, Damen Hague, intervened. Despite being fully aware of the truth, he introduced them to the court as a couple who intended to scam Richard! And they all managed to escape the law. Clara committed suicide after that due to severe distress and severe depression caused by her being raped and left without any support from the court system. After Clara's suicide, Joshua, who sought revenge on them, was severely beaten by Damen and his gang member friends. Joshua then tried to inform and convince Richard's wife, Dr. Sara Grinstein, of the incident and asked her for help. But my son did not know that they were complicit! This infernal couple tricked him! He was then slaughtered while alive. His body was found the next day next to a trash can. And his organs were sold on the black market.

Richard, Randall, Jonathan, Damen, Dane, and Sara formed a criminal gang of human traffickers who also worked with gangsters and various other criminals. After brutally raping and torturing their victims, they removed their organs in an underground clinic in the country house they jointly bought and then either sold them to the black market through their criminal contacts or performed organ transplants for their clients there. They met monthly and talked about their business. Of course, I know that you were not aware of the existence of that country house and that clinic and never went there. That's why there is a flash memory in the envelope. This flash memory contains all the evidence that proves what I said. It also contains all the photos and videos of their meetings and crimes and Jonathan's handwritten notes of all the events he did not attend but heard the details from others. There is also evidence of money transfers by their clients who purchased the organs. The address and CCTV footage of that country house and that underground clinic are included in that flash memory.

There is also an audio file named 'Clara' in there. It was recorded during the time Richard and Randall were raping her. It's the same file Jonathan took from them so that Richard and Randall could escape the law. I have to say that for personal reasons, there is no evidence of Joshua in there. Overall, as far as my research shows, they sacrificed twenty-seven innocent people, including children between the ages of ten and fifteen. These were also young men and women that were killed through brutal torture. Then your friends made money by selling their victims' organs. I followed them day and night for four years. The result of my research is the evidence in this flash memory.

Of course, I do not like you to look at its contents and hurt your beautiful soul. But I also can not let you suffer because of your lack of knowledge about their sudden absence. So, I wrote this letter just for you and put that flash memory in that envelope to prove my point. If you have any doubts, refer to it. But I repeat that it is better not to see its contents. Today, after realizing who I am and that I know the full story of their crimes, they immediately fled and went to Cuba on a private plane. Of course, I must say that you should not waste your time looking for them because there is no trace of them left to find them. I know very well that their actions never infected you, and you were completely unaware. So, I repeat, my dear daughter, be careful not to get caught up in people's deceptive appearances and not to be deceived by them. I arranged for all their property and bank account balances to be transferred to you. All you have to do is go to the lawyer whose card is in the same envelope as the flash memory. He is waiting for you to do the transfer of assets for you. I suggest that you keep those documents secret for your own sake and do not share any specific details with the police. Because of these crimes' high sensitivity, you will surely be interrogated for a long time as one of the suspects.

Besides, after the police learn about these events, they will release these documents, your name, profile, and image to the news and press. This will cause you trouble in the future. Or rather, it will be difficult for you to continue living in the community. I sincerely do not want any trouble for you. And I never released these documents to the press or the police to protect your reputation. Although many of the victims' families who lost their loved ones could finally have closure if they knew what happened to their loved ones, my preference is not to turn you into another victim. Go on with your beautiful life and forget that you knew these rubbish people. You are more valuable than to risk your life for those people for even a moment. I believe that you are a strong person and that you will not let this situation change you into what you are not.

Sincerely yours,

Dr. Ghiaccio Umanita.'

Johnna stood up as she began to read the letter. But when she reached the middle of the letter, her knees went weak, and she had to sit on the sofa to read the letter to the end. On the one hand, Johnna could not believe one word in that letter. On the other hand, all of those statements in the letter were, in a way, a response to the daily events of her life. Suddenly, she remembered that her husband told her once about a medical practice problem. One of Richard's patients and his wife sued them for their service. Johnna read the letter carefully once more and remembered something else.

Several years ago, they all went on a picnic and talked about buying a big farmhouse where they could keep horses. Because Johnna loved horses, she told them happily that she loved the idea, but they no longer talked about it! Even when Johnna brought it up again in another friendly gathering, everyone said, "No! this is a waste of money!" But she still did not believe that those people could commit such crimes!

However, the letter made things make sense. Randall used to disappear suspiciously and secretly for hours or even days. And it always

117

tormented Johnna like a great secret. Johnna knew that her husband was lying, but she did not know exactly what he was doing. When she asked questions, he would treat her violently, saying he had to stay in the hospital or go to another city for a conference and how dare she question him! She was very confused! She did not know how to feel about this whole thing; should she thank God that they did not harm her? Should she be afraid? Should she be ashamed for associating with these people? Or maybe this whole thing is a stupid prank?

However, Johnna decided not to do anything until the matter was completely clear. Then, she rushed through Richard and Sara's rooms to find a computer to review the contents of that flash memory. There was a computer inside the office. She hit the power button to turn it on, but it asked for the password! Johnna took a deep breath and moved out of the house, went to the parking lot, got in Randall's car, and left in a hurry to go back to her house and watch the flash memory's contents.

Her house was nearby. It was about two blocks away. After a short time, she got there and entered the house through the garage. Johnna rushed to the study, picked up her laptop, and turned it on. Then, she connected the flash memory to it and, as a habit, copied all the folders inside the flash drive to her laptop so that important information would not be lost. After a few moments, she opened the folder and saw the content. As soon as she saw the names of the files, dizziness and weakness came over her. She could no longer even believe what her eyes were seeing.

Now Johnna believed that the letter was from a benevolent and compassionate person. As he wrote, he was sympathetic to her suffering and wrote the letter like a father for his daughter. Thinking about Ghiaccio calmed her heart and gave her a lot of courage. She now knew one thing, and that was to thank God! She said to herself,

> "It does not matter how much it will bother and torment me to see these documents! It is important to know exactly what the truth is. As the saying goes, what does not kill you, will make you stronger! As Ghiaccio said in his letter, I am a strong woman! So, I can face the truth!"

Then, she took a few deep breaths to calm herself down. After that, she started from the first file and went on. Seeing those brutal and criminal scenes, she was shocked and started crying. Clara's audio file was utterly unbelievable to her.

She put her head on the table and started crying loudly, and raised it after a while, and followed the story. She came to the boy's video file whose finger was broken. Her husband tortured and then raped the little boy. Randall recorded the video as a trophy, which Jonathan obtained while everyone was in the country house. After watching the video for a few minutes, Johnna ran to the bathroom, lifted the toilet seat, threw up, sat in the bathroom for a little while, and then went to the refrigerator and carelessly picked up a sweet drink. After returning to the study, she sat behind her laptop and opened her drink. Before taking a sip, the image of the victims appeared in front of her eyes. Johnna closed her eyes with exhaustion, put her head on the table, and fell asleep. She woke up after thirty minutes and lifted her head. At first, she thought that all this was a bad dream, but after looking at the monitor, she realized that everything was real. Johnna read Jonathan's notes. After about an hour of reading those notes and constantly sobbing, utter despair overcame her. She felt deeply sympathetic to the victims and their families and decided to do everything in her power to alleviate their suffering. She knew Ghiaccio advised her not to cause trouble for herself. Still, her awakened conscience would not calm down and ignore the matter for her self-interest, while others were suffering from the loss of their loved ones. Johnna could not be silent and violate the rights of others. In her opinion, this was the least right of the victims and their families to know what happened. So, she picked up the phone and called 911. A few seconds later, the police dispatchers answered,

"It's 9.1.1. What is your emergency?"

"I want to…" Johnna paused for a moment, took a deep breath, then continued, "I want to report a series of crimes. But I do not know how to explain them. I do not know the terms for them!"

"This is okay. Do not worry about anything. First, I will ask you a few questions; please answer. Are you in a safe place?" asked the dispatcher.

"Yes, I am in a safe place," replied Johnna.

"Is there any immediate threat to you?" asked the dispatchers.

"No, I'm alone in my house," replied Johnna.

"May I ask your full name, please?" asked.

"My name is Johnna Hershberger," said Johnna.

"Okay, Johnna, please you tell me what happened?" asked the dispatcher.

"I accidentally found out today that my husband and five of our friends were involved in the murder of twenty-eight children, women, and men!" Johnna replied as she cried, "I have the names of the victims. I can read them for you, so you know I'm not kidding!"

"Yes, yes, please!" said the dispatcher.

Johnna began to read the names of the twenty-seven people. Then she took a deep breath and cleared her throat, and said,

"Twenty-six of them are missing persons. There was a 28-year-old woman that committed suicide four years ago because of these people's actions, and her name is Clara. But I do not know her last name. The last one was Clara's fiancé, Joshua, whose body was found in a trash can four years ago. His limbs were also reportedly amputated. I received an envelope today that contained a flash memory. It has all the videos and descriptions and documents about these crimes!"

The dispatchers said, "It's good that you called us! Would it be okay if I put you on hold for a few moments?"

"Yes, I will wait!" said Johnna.

"Please stay on the line!" said the dispatcher.

He then turned off his microphone and eagerly told his supervisor aloud, "Someone is on the phone and has detailed information about twenty-eight murders and the killers! I checked some of the names, and they are missing people!"

His supervisor jumped from his chair as if he's seen a ghost and said, "Keep her on the line and dispatch her information! Get as much information as you can!" He then ran out of the room quickly!

The dispatchers asked Johnna respectfully, "Is this your address, ma'am?" He read the address to Johnna.

"Yes! That is my address, and I am at the same address right now!" replied Johnna.

"Could you tell me the names of your spouse and friends?" asked the police dispatcher.

"Yes. My husband's name is Dr. Randall Hershberger. His friends are Dr. Richard Grinstein and his wife, Dr. Sara Grinstein, and Jonathan Hodge, and Damen Hague and his wife, Dane Hague," replied Johnna.

"Lieutenant Jonathan Hodge?!" asked the police dispatcher with great surprise.

"Yes! Lieutenant Jonathan Hodge! There are videos of his crimes!" replied Johnna.

"Do you know their whereabouts?" asked the police dispatcher.

"Yes! They allegedly fled to Cuba by a private plane!" said Johnna.

"How did you get this information?" asked the police dispatcher.

Johnna replied as if fainting, "I'm sorry, I'm not feeling well, I can't talk much longer! I think I have a panic attack, and I need a doctor!"

"Okay, don't hang up! If you can leave the front door open, then lie down on the floor. If you cannot get close to the front door, just lie on the floor wherever you are! The police will be there in three minutes! An ambulance is on its way too!"

Johnna barely made it to the front door and opened the door. Then, she laid down on the floor and fainted! About three minutes later, a large number of police cars surrounded the house. They immediately found Johnna and checked her vital signs.

121

Chapter 12

In the basement, after Ghiaccio and his assistants left and went upstairs, Jonathan quickly leaned forward, pulled the key forward with his head from the middle of the table, and opened his hands. He then threw the key in front of Richard, and he opened his hands and placed the key in front of Dane. After Dane opened her hands, she gave the key to Randall, not her husband! And Randall gave the key to Damen after opening his hand. After Damen unlocked his handcuffs, he threw the key in front of Sara, and she opened her hands too. Considered her death certain, Sara tried to make everyone pessimistic about the game,

"Look, this is a death game, and no one will come out of it alive! He wants us to kill each other in terrible ways! And in the end, he will kill the only survivor!"

"So far, he's done everything he said! You are the one who had an affair with my close friend after living together all those years! It was you who came up with the idea of removing Ghiaccio's son's organs! It was you who came up with the idea for the underground clinic! You are the only one who is not allowed to have an opinion anymore!" said Richard angrily.

"Yes, we never wanted to do this before the boy was killed! My only crime was taking bribes and sleeping with prostitutes! It was you and Damen who were in contact with the organ trafficking gang. Now, we will all burn because of your sins! And even now that Ghiaccio has given us a chance to escape, you want to take it away from us! Because you know very well that you and Richard are the only ones who can't get out of here alive because you killed his son with your own hands! Damn, the day I met you! I was a believer, a good person! But now I have become a criminal!" said Jonathan.

"You are only saying this because you know Ghiaccio is listening and are hoping maybe he'll change his mind about you!" said Damen, "You are the same person who tortured prostitutes close to the point of death when you had sex with them and gladly told me all about it! Even I, your friend, was surprised sometimes by the severity of your cruelty! And you are saying you have suddenly changed?! Aren't we all sinners?! We survived 100 times. This once, we barked up the wrong tree! and we are here now, and there is nothing we can do but to do what Ghiaccio says!"

"Now that Ghiaccio saw my video with that kid, what do you think will happen to me?!"

Randall asked in a frightened tone as if his heart was going to stop out of fear! He said this as if he had no hope of salvation!

"I honestly don't know what awaits us, but whatever it is, it must be very scary!" said Richard, "I never thought my ending would be in such a place!"

Ghiaccio, who was watching them upstairs through the camera, smiled and shook his head and said to his assistants,

"If they are given new chances a thousand more times, they will still commit the same crimes! With the difference that the number of victims will be 28,000, not 28!"

They waited anxiously for the right door to open. Suddenly a bang-sound came from the left door. A few moments later, the same sound came from the right one! Dane reached for the handle on the left door to check it; it opened! She looked at the others with surprise and said,

"It opened! This is the door that leads outside! They must have pressed the button by mistake! Let's run quickly before they understand that we are fleeing!"

"Close that door before you get us all killed!" shouted Jonathan.

Richard immediately went to the door to take a look outside! There was a long corridor with two doors at the beginning and end. Richard said to the crowd happily,

"Let's run fast! It looks like it doesn't have a camera either!"

Everyone except Jonathan got up from their chairs to take a look! They were all happy to see the bright corridor! Randall left the room and checked the entrance door in the hallway. They were locked. He turned to the crowd and said,

"Surely the one at the end of the hallway is the exit door! It probably goes to the seventh room that Ghiaccio said we could use to get out! Let's go!"

Jonathan went to the right door and opened it. It was dark, and he couldn't see anything. Suddenly, he got scared! He went back inside and said to the others,

"Let's go here together, as Ghiaccio said!"

Sara turned to Jonathan and said, "You idiot! We found a way out, and you are standing there?! Do you want to go to the slaughterhouse like a sheep?! Let's go quickly! They must have pressed the wrong button! We can go and surprise and defeat them! There are no cameras in the hallway, which means it was not designed for us! It was as if they had no plans for this! When he comes and sees we are gone, he will surely get angry and will kill you!"

Jonathan got scared after hearing what Sara said! What if she was right?! Jonathan hurried to the left door and left the room with others. After a few steps, the door closed, and suddenly a clicking sound came out of the door that showed it got locked! Jonathan rushed to see if the door was locked, and it was! Suddenly, he saw a camera and a speaker hidden behind the door when it was opened! Frightened, he shouted and said,

"Damn all of you! We all perished! I knew I shouldn't have listened to you! Now the way back is closed!"

Ghiaccio gave his assistants a meaningful look and said, "Well, as I expected! They chose the wrong path again! The plan starts as scheduled!"

In the corridor of the basement, everyone saw that camera and gasped for air out of fear! It felt like they were deceived! Ghiaccio began to speak through the speaker,

"After listening to you, I thought, what would they do if they were given a second chance?! I thought to myself, could they do as I told them?! I thought maybe at least one of you would follow the rules this time, especially after hearing what Jonathan said to Sara! I opened the left door for you so that you can choose! That was your second chance to make the right choice! The door on the left looked bright; it looked like somewhere with no camera and seemed like I didn't plan for you to be there, as Sara thought! But you saw that it has a camera and I did predict it! But the door on the right was an unknown and dark path, which in fact could have led to freedom for all of you! It's just like our daily lives! You were told to enter only through the right door, but I also gave you the ability to select the left door! And you still chose to go the wrong way against the rules of the game! That's why you entered the "game with human life!" And it was entering through the left door that got you into the game to start with!

Knowing that you will always choose the wrong path, as usual, I wanted you to face your true selves! Again, you consciously decided to break the law with full awareness! And you, Jonathan, you seemed to realize that you lost your way before but found yourself this time, so I gave you a second chance! But again, you got captivated by the temptations of this woman, Sara, and you ruined your life!"

Jonathan clenched his fist to hit Sara in the face in his anger when suddenly Ghiaccio said through the speaker,

"Be careful! You are in the game now! Be careful not to break the rules! Now, only one door is open to you, and that is the door in front of you. There are five walkie-talkies on the table at the end of the hall. They are one-way, only receiving my messages! The name of the owner is written on the back of each of them. I hear your voice everywhere in this building, so you do not need to send messages. Pick them up and put the earphones in your ears."

They went forward, and each took a walkie-talkie and looked at its back, swapping them together so that everyone could have their own.

"Each of you hears my voice privately," said Ghiaccio, "I will communicate with you separately at each step. So, pay attention to the instructions!"

"But I do not have a walkie-talkie!" said Dane.

"You will talk to me like you are doing now!" replied Ghiaccio.

"If this door does not end in freedom, then how would the right door end in freedom?" asked Damen.

Ghiaccio replied with a pause, "By choosing the right path, you would've first walked twenty-one yards. Then, you would've gone through a door and walked another nineteen yards. And twenty yards after that, you would have seen the door to freedom! Just like the years you've spent in your life!"

"So, you lied to us?! You broke the rules of the game!" said Richard.

"Lying?! Think a little bit to remember! What was the first time you broke a rule or a law? Maybe you cheated on your exam; maybe you stole something from someone; maybe you slandered others out of jealousy; or anything else. In all those moments, when you were thinking of breaking the law, things appeared to you in such a way that you thought that was the end of the road for you and that there was no hope anymore! You thought if you do not cheat, you will fail that exam; if you do not slander or harm that person, he will surely take your place; or if you do not steal that thing, you will become poor! And all those fears caused you to go down the stairs in the basement of your life! I just scared you in the basement, and I pictured a fair consequence for your crimes! You could have chosen the right path this time, but for fear of facing the reality of your actions, you chose the wrong path, again!" said Ghiaccio.

Then came the sound door being unlocked, which they had to go through.

"I repeat because you used to commit your crimes together, now you have to compete! Only one of you will come out of this basement alive, and that is the one who will obey my commands to the last step!" said Ghiaccio, "Of course, betraying each other is not a difficult task for any of you! You've done it many times before! You are all wild beasts! Now, enter the room and close the door behind you. You have forty-five minutes to complete each stage."

They all entered the room in fear, and the door closed behind them. Everyone was told in the headphones,

"At this stage, you either defeat Dane according to my order, or she escapes from your clutches, and you know the end of it! You have a specific time to complete this step. There are leather whips on the chair next to the wall. Grab them and hit her until I command you to stop. Make sure you do not hit her in the head!"

They took a deep breath and looked at each other very anxiously. Dane was very scared because she could hear the buzzing of the headphones. She could see that everyone was walking towards the chair. Then, she shouted,

"What is happening?! What do you want to do with me?!"

After picking up the whips, they attacked Dane from all sides and hit her. She fell to the ground as he screamed for help. Everyone seemed to think of nothing but themselves after the first blows. They thought they must do everything as Ghiaccio told them to survive and that If Dane were in their shoes, she would've done the same!

Indifferent to her friends' fate, she had asked Ghiaccio to release only her because she had no role in his son's murder. But now, it was her friends who were indifferent to her fate! Ghiaccio issued a stop order after 5 minutes.

He then told Damen to break the same finger that she broke on that little boy's hand. Damen didn't want to do that but bent down and took her finger in his hand, looked at Dane, and said, "Forgive me!" Then he twisted her finger firmly in the opposite direction. Everyone heard the sound of her bones breaking. Dane screamed and cried and begged.

Ghiaccio then told Jonathan to grab her by the neck and squeeze it to suffocate her and told him not to let go of her neck until Ghiaccio ordered to stop. Jonathan then sat on the floor next to her on his knees, grabbed her neck with both hands, and squeezed it with all his might. Dane's face turned red, and she started moving her arms and legs in the air to find a way to escape. The sound of her gasping for air upset everyone! Less than a minute later, Ghiaccio said stop, and Jonathan let go of her throat. Dane started coughing heavily and gasped for air.

Ghiaccio said to Dane, "Well, tell me, how does it feel when you feel completely helpless, and someone you once liked grabbed and squeezed your throat? Tell me, how did it feel when your finger broke, and there was nothing you could do?! Tell me, how did it feel when stronger people hit you?!"

> "Forgive me!" said Dane as she was crying and coughing, "Have mercy on me!"

> "Only those you hurt and tortured can forgive you, not me!" Ghiaccio said over the loudspeaker, "All I can do is stop you from suffering more!"

> Then he said in Richard's ear, "Sit on her chest and squeeze her throat, so she no longer moves!" He reluctantly did so. Dane shuffled and scratched Richard with her nails and wounded his face and arms.

After a few minutes, Dane did not move anymore! Damen began to cry! Ghiaccio saw on his monitor that the number in front of Dane's heart symbol turned zero. This meant that her heart did not beat anymore. He said in the speaker,

> "Now you can put her body on that chair!" They did so, and then the sound of the other door opening filled the air.

> "Now you enter the next step. Leave all the equipment in this room and go to the next room," said Ghiaccio.

Sara was terrified. Her whole body was shaking because she could guess what awaited her. She thought that if they went to the operating room, she should immediately find a razor or a surgical instrument and hit all of them in the neck! When they entered the room, they saw a hook attached to a chain hanging from the ceiling. The door behind them closed. Ghiaccio announced to everyone except Randall that he is the target at this point.

> "There is a handcuff on the chair in the right corner. Use that to tie his hands behind him and attach the handcuff to the hook to hang him from the ceiling. If you do not succeed, he will win this stage!" said Ghiaccio.

Randall realized that everyone was listening to Ghiaccio except him, so he knew that he was the target now. Jonathan immediately went to the handcuffs and picked them up. In order not to be surrounded, Randall turned his back to the wall.

> "If you come near me, I will break your teeth!" Randall told them and started punching and kicking aimlessly! Ghiaccio said in Jonathan and Damen's ears, "Attack him from both sides at

the same time and kick his knees very hard so that he falls to the ground!"

Then Jonathan ran to him from the right and Damen from the left, and they simultaneously kicked him hard in both knees and threw him to the ground. Jonathan immediately sat on his back, brought his hands behind his back, and handcuffed him. Then, they lifted Randall from the ground and hung the chains of the handcuff on the hook. Ghiaccio raised the hook slightly so that his feet would barely touch the ground. Randall tried to connect his toes to the ground, so the pressure on his wrists would be reduced, and the unbearable pain would be eased a little. He felt a sharp pain in his hands as they turned in the opposite direction, and he was screaming non-stop. Ghiaccio lifted the hook until he was completely off the ground. Ghiaccio then told Richard to punch him hard in the face to silence him. Richard did that, and Randall fell silent after the third punch and just moaned softly.

"Do you remember harassing children?!" Ghiaccio asked him through the speaker, "Do you remember anesthetizing Clara and raping her? Do you remember punching and slapping your wife in the face? It was because of you that Clara committed suicide. It was because of you that my son was killed. Remember those cigarette burns on the body of that child? And he was shouting and calling for his mother? And you videotaped his moans and cries!"

Ghiaccio told Richard to turn back and pick up a knife from behind a chair. Ghiaccio told Richard to take the knife and tear Randall's pants and shirt with it. He picked up the knife and returned to Randall, and started tearing up his clothes. Sara was excited to see the knife! She wanted to grab and hide it and defend herself with it when they attacked her! After tearing Randall's clothes, Ghiaccio told Richard to give the knife to Sara. Ghiaccio then asked Sara to remove Randall's Achilles tendons. Sara hurriedly grabbed the knife and bent down to carry out the order. After cutting his leg tendons, he screamed and cried a lot. Ghiaccio then told her to cut the tendons in Randall's knee from behind. And Sara did it right away. He then told her,

"Because of Clara's age, which was 28 years old, and the total number of victims, which was also 28, cut 28 pieces out of his skin, each the size of a palm!"

When Sara started doing that, Randall started screaming terribly. Ghiaccio lowered the hook slightly so that he could stand on his feet. But because his tendons were cut off, his feet could not hold his body's weight and started swinging around like a puppet. Ghiaccio told Damen to punch him in the chin repeatedly to silence him. Damen started punching Randall in the face. He fell silent after a few blows. Blood was coming out of his mouth. Ghiaccio told Damen, "If he starts screaming again, keep hitting him until he gets quiet!" Unable to bear the pain anymore, Randall begged Ghiaccio with the same bloody mouth, "Please kill me, have mercy on me!" Ghiaccio took a deep breath and told Richard to go to the place where he picked the knife. He told Richard to pick up a syringe this time.

"Take it and inject Randall with it!"

It was an anticoagulant syringe so Randall would die slowly from bleeding, just like Clara! Richard immediately went there, grabbed the syringe, and then turned to Randall. As Sara was peeling Randall's skin, Richard injected him with the syringe. After Sara finished cutting out 28 pieces of Randall's skin, she counted the wounds to make sure the number is right! Ghiaccio then told Sara to insert the knife up to the handle in his abdomen below his navel and then leave it there and not pull it out. Sara was upset to hear that because she wanted to take the knife with her secretly. Disappointed, she carried out the order, and Randall started screaming again. Damen immediately started punching him in the chin. Randall fell silent after a few blows. Blood was gushing out of his mouth as if the continued punches tore his tongue. Ghiaccio then lowered the hook, and Randall fell to the ground on his face. He told them to put his body on the chair in that room. They dragged his body to the chair and placed it there. Ghiaccio continued,

> "25 minutes have passed since you started this stage. If he does not die in the next 20 minutes, you will all lose, and Randall wins this game- even if he dies after the time is up!"

Everyone became extremely anxious! Randall had many serious wounds, but it did not look like he would die in 20 minutes!

> "You deliberately want us to lose!" Sara told Ghiaccio as she heard Randall moaning, "Otherwise, if I had known this from the beginning, I would have deepened his wounds, or I would make a bigger hole in his stomach so he would die sooner!"

Ghiaccio did not respond for 15 minutes. It was as if he could not hear them! Their anxiety was getting worse by the minute. They did not know what to do. They kept begging him to tell them what to do to survive! They were not allowed to touch Randall at all! Those fifteen minutes passed like fifteen years! Suddenly, Ghiaccio told Jonathan to gently pull the knife out of Randall's abdomen and cut the vein on his wrist. Jonathan did as he was told, and Randall died slowly after about four minutes of heavy bleeding.

Chapter 13

After Randall died, the door to the next room opened, and Ghiaccio told them to go there. When they entered, Ghiaccio just told Jonathan that there was a chair on the right side,

"Go there and pick up a gun from behind that chair. It has two bullets in it."

Ghiaccio immediately told Richard in his ear to go straight ahead and turn back when he reached the wall. He then told Jonathan that he should hit Richard in the area below the navel with those two bullets as soon as he turned back. Jonathan shot him when he turned back! The sound of gunfire echoed through the room so intensely that their ears began to ring. The sound was so loud that Damen and Sara were completely shocked. Richard felt someone kicked him very hard and fell to the ground. He felt severe pain and an intense burning sensation in his lower abdomen. He felt that someone was pulling out his intestines and began to scream in fear and put his hand on the inflicted area and cried in agony. Damen and Sara did not know if it was their turn next to be shot, so both of them suddenly attacked Jonathan and punched and kicked him!

"Wait!" said Jonathan, who was under their fists and kicks, "Wait! I just executed the command! The victim of this stage is Richard! I should have done that! This weapon has no more bullets!"

Damen and Sara stopped. They were exhausted and were breathless! Ghiaccio then told Sara to go to the chair. There is a syringe behind it. Take it and inject Richard with it. Sara went and picked it up and walked over to Richard. He was still rolling on the ground in pain. She tried to inject it, but Richard kept punching and kicking and begging them not to kill him.

Ghiaccio told Damon to sit on Richard's feet so he could not move. He then told Jonathan to hold his hands so Sara could inject him. Richard's bleeding intensified after Sara injected him. Ghiaccio told Damen that he would start counting from one to twenty-eight, and with the count of each number, Damen must strike a strong punch on Richard's bullet wound. Then he started counting,

"One. Two. Three. Four. Five .... Twenty-eight!"

Richard's screams echoed in the room with every punch, and he was remembering everything in shock. Damen was completely tired and was waiting for the count to end. Ghiaccio said to Richard,

> "Do you feel the pain?! It's like Clara's pain and the other women you preyed on while they were completely defenseless! Here are the very people you trusted and with whom you committed crimes. For their salvation, one of them shot you, another one injected you so your bleeding wouldn't stop, and the other eagerly punched you!"

Ghiaccio then told them to place Richard's body on the chair in the room. Richard died after about fifteen minutes. After Ghiaccio saw on his monitor that his heart rate dropped to zero, he opened the door to the next room. Jonathan dropped the gun. They knew full well that they had to enter. Damen's hands were bloody. Sara moved like a corpse. She found the room completely dark. Ghiaccio told the other two to enter the room and close the door behind them. Upon entrance, they realized they could hardly see anything. Ghiaccio then told Jonathan and Damen that the victim of this room would be either Sara or the two of them because there are tools that Sara will surely use if she sees them! Then he said,

> "In a few moments, lights will be turned on, and you have to catch Sara before she makes a move. If she escapes, it will become very difficult to catch her! She is standing in front of you with her back to you."

As they were getting ready, suddenly the lights came on. When Sara saw a surgical bed behind a medical partition in a corner, she immediately realized that it was her turn! With little light shining through from the previous room, she did not see the bed at all when she entered. She wanted to flee from the other side but suddenly and unknowingly fell into Damen and Jonathan's hands. She was struggling and throwing punches and kicks in the air to release herself. Jonathan slapped her savagely, and held her hands with one arm, and held her hair tightly with the other. Damen wrapped his arms around her. She jumped up and down like a fish out of water! She tried to hit Jonathan with her feet, but Jonathan lifted her by her hair, knocked her to the ground, and pressed her head to the floor. Ghiaccio told them to put her on the bed,

> "You should tie her hands and feet to the wristbands attached to the bed for this purpose!"

Sara tried to escape and release her head from Jonathan's grip. Damen suddenly punched her in the chin and disoriented her. Jonathan then threw one hand around Sara's neck and pressed her tightly to his side, then locked the hand holding her neck with his other hand. Then, he got up from the floor, picked her up, and went to the bed's left side. As soon as Sara tried to punch and kick, Jonathan put more pressure on her neck so she would give in under the pressure of suffocating!

Jonathan then told Damen to first tie her right hand to the left side of the bed and then lift her left foot and tie it to the bottom wristband. Damen did it right away. Jonathan told him to push the bed from the corner to the middle of the room to open up space on the bed's right side. Damen immediately pushed the bed and took it to the middle of the room.

"I want to put you on the bed!" Jonathan told Sara, still holding her neck tightly, "If you resist, your arms and legs will be broken! Do you understand?"

Sara could not say a word as Jonathan kept his hand on her mouth, so she just nodded in agreement. Jonathan then told Damen,

"Whenever I turn her on the bed, you immediately lock her hand!"

"Okay!" said Damen.

Then, as Jonathan held Sara's neck, he approached the bed and first threw Sara on the bed, forced her to turn, and then fell on her to keep her still. Sara's other hand was in the air in front of Damen, and he tied her other hand to the bed. Because Sara had one arm and one leg tied to the bed, she had to turn so that her arms and legs would not break. Damen then tied the one leg that was free to the bed, looked at Jonathan, and they both took a deep breath. They were exhausted! Sara cursed them non-stop!

Ghiaccio told Damen, "There are a knife and a ball gag to block Sara's mouth on the chair next to the wall. Grab them. Give the knife to Jonathan and put the ball in her mouth!"

Sara followed Damen's moves with her eyes. When she saw the knife in his hand, she started screaming and shaking the bed with her body. When Damen approached her, she began to beg and said,

"Please, Please, do not kill me! I do not want to die like this here! At least shoot me. Please, I'm begging you!"

Damen shoved the ball in Sara's mouth tightly as she begged. Only some incomprehensible sounds could be heard from Sara. Jonathan, who was very angry with Sara for everything, asked Ghiaccio,

"How much time have we spent so far?"

Ghiaccio replied, "Twenty minutes!"

"I do not know if I can get out of here alive, but let me hurt her a little bit!" Jonathan said, "Because, without Sara, many of the crimes would not have happened!" Ghiaccio answered a little later,

"No, you cannot do anything other than what I tell you! It does not matter what she or anyone else has done to you! Your crime began when you listened to her invitations and temptations. The important thing was not to commit immoral acts, like Johnna. But now that you are in this basement with her, you cannot blame her. Rather, you were the one who committed all those crimes. You are fighting for your life, not for revenge. So, do what you have been told. Now, give that knife back to Damen!" Jonathan followed the order.

"Two leather straps are attached to the bed. One in the head area and the other in the navel area," Ghiaccio told Jonathan, "Take them out from under the mattress and tie them very tightly." Jonathan did it.

Ghiaccio then told Damen to grab the knife and tear off the front of Sara's dress. Damen did it. She was fainting from fear and could not even move her head or the middle of her body. She was moaning with her eyes bulging out of their sockets. Ghiaccio told her through a speaker,

"Do you remember that you tore my child to pieces without anesthesia and used non-surgical knives to stage his torture? Then you took out his organs and sold them. This is going to be the same feeling and pain that he experienced. Now taste your own medicine!"

Ghiaccio told Damen and Jonathan, "Damen, show her the knife, and then very slowly, cut through her chest from seven inches below her neck, right in the middle, right through her navel. Remember to cut only the outer layers. Her organs must remain intact. When you start cutting, you will only have less than four minutes to finish the procedure correctly. After that, she will surely die or at least lose consciousness. If the latter happens, then you will lose! If you lose, you will be the next person on that bed! Jonathan should help you open the cut using his hands. First, you take out her kidneys and separate them. Then, you have to take out her heart while it is beating and cut its veins!"

With trembling hands, Damen examined the start and endpoints. Then, he stretched his hand back and forth linearly on those points several times. He started cutting after that. The sound of moans and screams coming from Sara's closed mouth tormented him. With a few tries and passing the knife through the cutting path, he finally removed skin, fat, and flesh layers. Sara's body was bleeding profusely and was shaking from the pain and pressure drop. Jonathan reluctantly pulled and opened both sides of the incision on her torn abdomen.

"It's full of blood here. I don't see anything!" Damen said stressfully, "I do not know where the kidneys are!"

"Cut a piece of the mattress and use its sponge to dry the blood!" said Ghiaccio.

Damen quickly cut a corner of the mattress, removed the cover, and put the sponge inside to absorb the blood. Then, he took out the sponge and said, "I see them now!"

He took her kidneys by hand, separated them from the fat layers, and then cut them out with a knife. Sara's eyes were closing. Damen hurriedly shouted to Jonathan to open the area quickly. Jonathan began to vomit from the scene and the smell of blood. Damen shouted again and told Jonathan,

"Her eyes are closing! Hurry up!"

Jonathan grabbed the top of her chest while disgusted and nauseous and opened it with great pressure. Damen slowly pulled Sara's heart out of her chest as it pounded softly. Then, he looked into her half-closed eyes and quickly cut her veins. He took a deep breath. He lowered his head as if he was reviewing his memories with her. Then, he put her heart on her chest and took a few steps back. He sat down on the ground, took his head in his blood-stained hands, and wept.

Ghiaccio told them to put her body on a chair and place her heart and kidneys under her feet. They did exactly as they were told, then looked at each other bitterly and shook their heads.

Ghiaccio told Jonathan, "This is the final stage, and you have to kill Damen! After opening the door, you must first let Damen enter. Then you attack him from behind and knock him to the ground. Before attacking him, when you enter the room, there is a wristband right next to the door that you must take. Remember to tie his hands behind his back with the wristband!"

Ghiaccio then told Damen, "This is the final stage, and you have to kill Jonathan. When the door opens, you must enter first. When you enter, there is a stick in front of you near the wall. You have to pick it up and use it to attack Jonathan and kill him!"

When the door opened, Damen rushed in first to reach for the stick. Immediately after him, Jonathan entered and picked up the wristband from the floor. Damen was surprised to see that nothing was on the ground! He realized that Ghiaccio lied to him! When he turned, Jonathan punched him in the face and knocked him to the ground, then immediately tied his hands behind his back.

"You seem to be the winner of this game! Now go to the chair and take the fishing hooks attached to the threads!" Ghiaccio told Jonathan.

Jonathan went and picked them up. Then went back to Damen. Ghiaccio continued,

"First, turn him around, so he faces the ground. Stick the hook to the back of his pants. Then fold his legs and sit on them until your weight completely bends them. Tie the hook to the shackles of his legs."

Jonathan did exactly what Ghiaccio said. Damen did not move or protest or moan. He was in shock! He never thought Ghiaccio would fool him like that! Maybe if he knew, he would punch his friends less! Now it was his turn to shout and beg!

> Ghiaccio continued, "Take another hook and put it up inside his mouth. Pull the hook from behind the head so that it's completely bent backward and then tie it tightly to his waist!"

Again, Jonathan did exactly what Ghiaccio said. Suddenly, Damen came to his senses and shouted with a lot of stubbornness,

> "Ghiaccio, you are a dirty liar! You are not better than us, but worse than us!"

> "Now take another hook and put it in his mouth," Ghiaccio told Jonathan, ignoring Damen's words, "This time, pull it from the bottom of his jaw and fasten it to the shackles of his legs so that his mouth is left completely open. If he tries to close his mouth, he will surely open it again due to the pressure and pain!"

A little frightened by the intensity of Ghiaccio's violence and torture, Jonathan recalled Sara saying,

> "He will kill everyone in the end!"

He lied to Damen so Jonathan could win. "Maybe he did it on purpose. Apart from Dane, I had the least role in the killing of his child!" Jonathan thought to himself. Nevertheless, he had no choice but to do what Ghiaccio wanted.

> Ghiaccio continued, "Now, take the knife from behind the chair and tear the first hook and thread you tied to it!"

Jonathan went and picked up the knife from behind the chair and returned to Damen and tore that thread. After the thread was torn, Damen's legs opened slightly from the collapsed position, which opened his mouth to the end. Damen started screaming and crying in pain.

> "It's still a little early to shout!" said Ghiaccio, "The main show hasn't even started yet! Do you remember the time when you knowingly violated the rights of others in courts by bending the law with your tricks?! Do you remember that with complex legal games, you did not even allow others to defend themselves?! Do you remember how many lives were destroyed by your mouth and tongue?! Do you remember using your tongue to order your gangster friends to beat my son severely?

Do you remember negotiating the sale of my child's and many other children's organs with that tongue? Do you remember the other crimes you committed using your tongue? Now, YOU dare calling me a liar?!"

He then sent down the hook that hung near the ceiling at the push of a button and told Jonathan to attach that large iron hook to the shackles of Damen's foot. Jonathan did it, and Ghiaccio lifted that big hook.

When Damen hung from his legs, his lower jaw broke with a horrible sound and clung to his chest. A hook attached to his lower jaw in his mouth first broke his teeth, then tore his lower lip. Because his jawbone was broken in the middle, his mouth remained open and could not be closed. He was screaming so hard that the hair on Jonathan's neck stood up! Ghiaccio told Jonathan,

"Now take another fishing hook and stick it in his tongue. Then pass the thread through the metal ring that is attached to the wall behind you. Pull the thread tightly so that his body goes from vertical to horizontal. Then, tie it so that he stays horizontal!"

Jonathan thought to himself that Damen's death was worse than Sara's. He put the thread the way Ghiaccio wanted. Damen hung horizontally from his tongue for a moment until his tongue was torn and the hook came off. After becoming detached from the hook, he swung like a pendulum while hanging from his legs. Damen was bleeding profusely from his mouth and was screaming in pain. Ghiaccio told Damen through the speaker,

"If you think the name of this condition is pain, then you still don't know what pain awaits you, Mr. Lawyer!"

Ghiaccio then told Jonathan, "There is a syringe in the back of the chair. Take it and inject him with it in the vein of his neck!"

All the veins in Damen's neck were protruded because of them hanging from his legs for a while, and it was very easy to inject something into them. The solution inside was a highly toxic poison obtained from a mammal called Platypus. Its property was to induce hyperalgesia.

Hyperalgesia is a disease in which people develop an abnormally increased sensitivity to pain. The pain that results from this poison stays in people's systems even for weeks. Moreover, this poison does not reach the body's natural painkillers. In a short time, it causes more pain in the body than firing a bullet. The various substances in this poison have different effects on the body, such as a severe drop in blood pressure, a quick increase in pain in the affected and injured areas, a quick increase in the blood flow, and the loss of the body's ability to stop bleeding. Normally, injecting this poison alone cannot kill a person, but it can lead to temporary painful paralysis. Ghiaccio used this poison for Damen because it enhanced the process of feeling pain by affecting how pain signals were processed in the brain and spinal cord and prevented blood from clotting. After injecting the solution, Ghiaccio told Jonathan,

"There are still 15 minutes until the end of this stage for the exit door to open!"

Looking forward to his release, Jonathan felt that he was the happiest man on earth because he was the only one who could survive! He waited impatiently for Damen to die and for himself to be released! After 10 minutes of screaming in pain and making heartbreaking noises, Damen suddenly suffered a brain shock due to the intensity of the pain. Therefore, he had a strong seizure. As he was going through the seizure, Ghiaccio told Jonathan to cut the vein on his neck. Exhausted by all this, Jonathan grabbed the knife and did it. Damen's heart stopped forever after less than two minutes. After he died, Ghiaccio lowered the large metal hook and said,

"Now he's dead. Put him on a chair!"

After 15 minutes of waiting, which felt like 15 years for Jonathan, he heard Ghiaccio's voice, which sounded like a liberating voice! Jonathan thought to himself that because Ghiaccio had so much evidence of his and his friends' crimes, he would no longer be afraid to report them to the police about the incidents and murders that took place there. Jonathan was so tired that he could barely move Damen. But he did so with full enthusiasm and put him on the chair. Then, the door opened! His eyes fell on Ghiaccio as his two assistants accompanied him on his left and right sides. He entered the room with a happy smile!

"You are one step away from freedom!" said Ghiaccio.

Jonathan breathed a sigh of relief! Ghiaccio pointed to the chair and said,

"There is a handcuff and a blindfold on the chair. Put the blindfold on your eyes. Then, grab the handcuffs and tie your hands from behind and sit on the chair, so we can get you ready to go!"

Jonathan thought to himself that they are doing this to keep their address and location hidden, so he eagerly followed Ghiaccio's instructions. Then, he heard people walking around the room and thought to himself that they are preparing for his departure!

Suddenly, he heard the sound of the hook coming down! The two assistants approached him, and one of them took off his blindfold! He saw in disbelief that a rope of execution was in front of him! He started panting,

"But you said you were a man of your word!" Jonathan said in a trembling voice, "You said you would release whoever gets to this stage!"

Ghiaccio laughed from the bottom of his heart and said, "It is true that hyenas are just wild, but they also have small brains! This is what you did to my child! Do you remember how you crushed his hope? Do you remember that you promised them that you would follow the story, but you did not? Do you remember that you took away their documents from them so that they could not defend their rights? As a policeman, you had to be on their side, but you betrayed them! Now, see what it tastes like to be disappointed and for all your hopes to perish! As a police officer, you must protect the interest and stability of society. But you were the most corrupt one, and instead, you threatened and damaged society's stability! You sacrificed the vulnerable women who turned to prostitution out of poverty and for food. One thing to remember: 'God did not create anyone as a prostitute, it's the men who distribute the loaves of bread in the town that leave women without it, so whenever they desire a woman, they can easily buy her for the price of a loaf of bread!'

Now is the time to truly experience the meaning of instability, insecurity, and fear of losing your life! I have been planning this for four years! Now, you see that the bitter gets bitten! Now, you see that you are not more intelligent than others!"

141

He took a deep breath and said triumphantly, "Sometimes a quick death is like a reward for some people! And the way you'll die is like a reward compared to the death of your friends!"

Ghiaccio pointed to his bodyguards. They lifted Jonathan and put a rope around his neck. Then, Ghiaccio used the tablet in his hand and raised the hook. One of the guards put a broken footstool under Jonathan's feet. Ghiaccio then pulled the hook so that only the tips of Jonathan's toes touched the footstool. Johnathan tried to put his weight on his legs to reduce his neck pressure. The footstool constantly trembled under his feet, and he kept moving from left to right and from right to left! Ghiaccio pulled the hook up and down several times. He didn't want Johnathan to die right away, but also didn't want him to breathe easily either! Then, he told Johnathan that this is what corrupt police do to people; they 'block people's airways!' After about fifteen minutes, suddenly, the footstool broke under Jonathan's feet, and he hung from the rope and died. Ghiaccio lowered the hook and said to his assistants,

"Put him on that chair! We will burn them all tomorrow morning!"

Ghiaccio went upstairs to his living room.

Chapter 14

Ghiaccio sat on his own dark red leather sofa with a large LED TV in front of him. He lifted the TV remote from the sofa handle and turned it on. He pulled forward a crystal glass from the side table on his right with his right hand. He grabbed his favorite whiskey bottle that was next to a picture of his wife, Joshua, and Clara, with his right hand and opened the lid with his left hand. Then, he poured some whiskey into the glass, and after closing the lid, he put the bottle in its place. He looked at his dead family's picture and smiled nostalgically. Then, he raised his glass to them and said, "Cheers!" He started watching TV, and the news that was being broadcast caught his attention. A picture of all the criminals killed in his house's basement was displayed on the television screen! At the bottom of the screen was written: 'The secret of the murders of at least twenty-six missing persons has been revealed by one of the suspects' wife"! He took the TV remote and turned up the volume,

"Today, we were informed by police public relations at an unexpected press conference that the identities of a criminal gang, including a police officer, a lawyer, three specialist doctors, and a schoolteacher, had been revealed," the anchor said anxiously, "We became aware that they were involved in human organ trafficking in collaboration with some gang groups. The names of this criminal gang are Dr. Randall Hershberger, Dr. Richard Grinstein, his wife Dr. Sara Grinstein, Lieutenant Jonathan Hodge, Damen Hague, attorney at law, and his wife, Dane Hague, a school teacher.

The police spokesman expressed his deepest condolences to the victims and their families. He said that Jonathan Hodge's shameful actions never represented law enforcement agencies. He said they would prove this by prosecuting all those who played the slightest role in this criminal gang's activities. Even those who bought organs from this criminal gang during this period are in the police department's custody."

The news anchor paused for a moment and then continued, "According to the latest news from the public relations of the police, these criminals fled to Cuba today through the air border, after learning of the disclosure of their activities. The police found their names in the manifesto of a private rental flight to Cuba.

Due to the large scale of this tragedy and the serial nature of the killings, the Federal Police has taken control of this investigation in cooperation with the Local Police Departments. Initially, the tragedy was reported by Johnna Hershberger, the wife of Dr. Randall Hershberger. According to police, Johnna Hershberger reached out to the police and did not have any prior knowledge about the crimes until today. Mrs. Hershberger told the police that today, all of them were anesthetized while they were guests at Dr. Richard Grinstein's house. After regaining consciousness, she noticed the absence of her husband and friends. After searching for them, she found a flash memory containing all the evidence of these crimes in detail in the form of videos, photos, audio, and text files that reveal the vast scope of this tragedy. She then immediately called the police. The flash memory was allegedly left to her when she was unconscious by a man who worked as a gardener in the house and whose identity is unknown to the police. According to the police, he left the evidence anonymously, wanting Mrs. Hershberger to report the crimes. According to the obtained documents, the police managed to identify and locate an illegal secret clinic belonging to this criminal group. The clinic is located in the basement of a country house about 100 miles outside the city. Forensics experts reported that after finding human remains, advanced surgical and transplant equipment, and the presence of a furnace used to burn corpses in the area, police fear they might have found a slaughterhouse in which criminals surgically transferred the organs. Of their victims to recipients."

The news anchor paused for a second and then said, "It seems that our colleagues have succeeded in establishing a visual communication line with Mrs. Hershberger!"

Then Johnna's beautiful and innocent face appeared on TV. It was clear from her face and eyes that she cried a lot. News anchor welcomed Johnna and thanked her for accepting their invitation. Johnna also gave a polite response.

"Mrs. Hershberger, I'm sorry for the tragedy that has happened around you!" said the anchor, "We heard that you weren't in a good state of mind after learning about these crimes and watching the videos, and you were taken to the emergency room. We hope you are well now! Can you tell us how you first found that flash memory?"

"Yes! When I woke up, I noticed the absence of others. When I was looking for them, I saw a flash memory next to me. At first, I thought the others went for a walk in the yard. I called my husband's cell phone. I was surprised to see that it was off. Then I called my mother to see if it was the end of the world! She picked up, and I realized there was no problem! I called the others who were with us at the party, and I was even more surprised to see that their phones were all turned off too. I rushed to my house. Then I thought to myself to look at the contents of that flash memory!" said Johnna.

Johnna was choked with tears and paused. She tried hard not to cry, but she couldn't control herself and cried innocently as she continued speaking,

"It was then that I realized I was living with a pack of wild animals that had no empathy and compassion! Their crimes were so gruesome that when I called 911, I did not know how to explain to them, so they'd believe me! I could not think of words to describe them!"

"Who do you think left that flash memory next to you?!" asked the news anchor with a sad expression, "Is it possible that it fell out of their pockets before they escaped?!"

"I cannot answer this accurately because I was completely unconscious!" replied Johnna, "But I think that kind gardener left me that flash memory so that I could release it to the police! Of course, given the power and influence of Lieutenant Jonathan Hodge in different parts of the city, the gardener must have wanted to be careful! They must have realized somehow that their secret was revealed, so they escaped!"

"Why do you think the gardener did that?!" asked the news anchor.

145

"I do not know. This was the first time I saw him!" said Johnna, "His name is Mr. Ghiaccio."

The news anchor asked in surprise, "Was his real name Ghiaccio?"

"Yes. He introduced himself in public with that name. Dr. Richard Grinstein said the gardener had only been working for him for a few months. He also said that he did not know Mr. Ghiaccio before hiring him. Mr. Ghiaccio told us a story before I fainted. During the story, he told us that he was a retired journalist and did gardening for fun. But I think he is the one who collected all this evidence. And he pursued these people for years. That's why he was gardening in their house. In my opinion, he is a real hero, but he wanted his identity to stay hidden!" Replied Johnna.

"I do not know much Italian, but Ghiaccio means ice!" said the news anchor, "I do not think it is a common name. Anyway, don't you think this is a little suspicious?! Why do you think he gave you these documents and not the police?!"

Johnna thought about it and then said passionately, "In my opinion, not only is it not suspicious, but it's very heroic! If you watch those videos and photos, you will realize what service he has rendered to the whole community by releasing those documents! These were beasts that lived among us, and nobody had any idea who they really were and what they did! They were butchering whoever came across their way. And in answer to your question as to why he gave me this information, I must say I am sure that he must have wanted to bring relief to the families of the victims by releasing these documents, but I do not know why he gave them to me and not the police. It could be out of fear of Jonathan's widespread influence and power!"

"Thank you for your presence and for accepting our invitation! In the end, if you have a word or message, please say it to the viewers of our program!" Said the news anchor, respectfully and friendly.

Johnna replied with tears, "I am very ashamed of having a connection to these people! I'm ashamed, and I'm sorry, from the bottom of my heart! I feel sympathy and grief for the victims and their families! The least I could do was to call the police immediately! I want to say to the victims' families that I know that money will never fill the hole left in their hearts! Still, I want them to know that all the property of these criminals is in my control now. This wealth is collected with the blood money of others. I want to give all of it to the victims' families to use it as they see fit. I hope, maybe, this would be a little relief for the deep wounds of their hearts."

Then, they displayed a picture of the twenty-seven victims on the screen and told their names one by one, except for Joshua's photo and information about him. There was no information about him in that flash memory. Johnna verbally told the police that a young man who was Clara's fiancé was killed four years ago. Ghiaccio turned off the TV. He put his empty whiskey glass on the table and refilled it halfway. Then he laughed happily and said,

"Bravo, good girl! I knew you would make me proud! I knew it!"

He started laughing again and shook his head in satisfaction, and drank some more whiskey. He said loudly,

"The only thing necessary for the triumph of evil is for good men to do nothing!"

Two days later, when Johnna felt better, she went to see the lawyer whose business card was in Ghiaccio's envelope. Johnna introduced herself. The lawyer asked how she found his address, and Johnna replied that a loved one gave her a business card with his address on it. The lawyer asked for the card, and Johnna gave it to him. He had turned all the white papers that the criminals signed into a power of attorney! Those documents granted complete control over all property and assets, and accounts to Johnna in case of their absence. Johnna asked him to sell all their property and even her house and car and put the money in a trust account in her name. She wanted to share the money equally between all the families of the victims. The lawyer willingly agreed to do this for her for free to contribute to the good deed. Johnna then made another request. She asked that lawyer to help her change her last name to Umanita. She wanted to get rid of any contact with those criminals and anything that reminded her of them.

"There is no problem!" said the lawyer, "It is a very good decision. I just need to write a new will with your new name for Dr. Paul Umanita!"

Johnna asked in surprise, "Excuse me? Who?"

"The same person who gave you my card!" said the lawyer, "He told me your name and took my business card for you! He drew a star mark on the back of the card with a red marker and showed it to me. He told me your name and details and said 'I will give this card to my beautiful daughter and she will come here! Help her in whatever she wants to do!' So, when you introduced yourself, and I asked you to show me the business card, I knew it was you he was talking about! He gave me those power of attorney papers yesterday and asked me to make a will for him and put your name as his sole heir! And I did that too. Now, when you change your name, I will change it in the will too. He also left a sealed envelope to give to you!"

The lawyer then opened a drawer, took out an envelope, and handed it to Johnna. She took it, thanked him, and left. She opened the envelope outside of the office. There was a letter inside:

"My beautiful daughter, Johnna!

I've known you for the past four years, right when I lost Joshua and was looking for his killers. I came across you when I was looking for Randall to gather evidence. At first, I thought that you are like the others because you lived under the same roof with such a criminal! But after installing cameras in your house, I accidentally saw your secret prayers to God! I listened to you carefully! I saw an angel there with a heart full of love for people! It was there that I learned the greatest lesson of my life, that I should never judge anyone too quickly, even in the most difficult times of life and in the most unacceptable matters! From that day on, the more I got to know you, the more embarrassed I became about my initial judgment of you! You are like a beautiful flower in this world! In my opinion, it is the inner beauty of people like you that makes life bearable with all its ugliness! From that day on, I did not seek revenge for my son, but my goal became saving you and others. I went from an angry father to a compassionate gardener. I said this so that whenever you think about why you were under the same roof with such people, remember what a great impact your inner beauty and kindness had on my life and goal!

I saw your TV interview. And I was proud of you as a father. Of course, I did not expect anything else from you! You passed the biggest test of your life, proudly! You preferred the comfort of others to your own! While you could only save yourself, you bent down to take the hand of others! You were not just kind to people in your prayers, but you proved it in practice! Although you had no hand in those tragedies and were not guilty, you humbly apologized to the victims' families in front of millions of people for associating with the criminals! You could at least make yourself a hero with the useful information you provided; However, you still tried to attribute the good deed to me! In my previous letter, I told you that it was only for you, so you did not abuse my trust and did not talk to anyone about that letter! Now, I think that you are the only one who deserves to be the heir of the Umanita family, and after my death, all my wealth will go to you!

The address of your new home is at the back of this letter. Loyal servants have been chosen to take care of you and help you with your work! They know you well and are waiting for you! Cars and a reliable driver are at your disposal to serve you 24 hours a day, seven days a week! Inside your private room, there is a safe box with the code 32437374. Please change the password to your liking. Inside that box is your new bank account with $10 million in it! Use it as you wish! Of course, a sum of money will be credited to your account by me, your father, every month!

There is also a mobile phone that is for your use only! In that, my direct and special number is saved under the name 'Dad' along with my address! I have also prepared a Hawaii tour package for you to get away from these catastrophes and relax! Of course, you fly there by private plane! Be sure to come to visit me sometime when you miss me! It will make me happy! Contact me anytime, anywhere, for anything you need!

Lovingly,

Dad"

[The End]

Printed in Great Britain
by Amazon